~Presents~

Don't miss out on any of our books in March!

This month, Lynne Graham brings you *The Italian Billionaire's Pregnant Bride,* the last story in her brilliant trilogy THE RICH, THE RUTHLESS AND THE REALLY HANDSOME, where tycoon Sergio Torrente demands that pregnant Kathy marry him. In *The Spaniard's Pregnancy Proposal* by Kim Lawrence, Antonio Rochas is sexy, smoldering and won't let relationship-shy Fleur go easily! In Trish Morey's *The Sheikh's Convenient Virgin,* a devastatingly handsome desert prince is in need of a convenient wife who must be pure. Anne Mather brings you a brooding Italian who believes Juliet is a gold-digger in *Bedded for the Italian's Pleasure.* In *Taken by Her Greek Boss* by Cathy Williams, Nick Papaeliou can't understand why he's attracted to frumpy Rose—but her shapeless garments hide a very alluring woman. Lindsay Armstrong's *From Waif to His Wife* tells the story of a rich businessman who avoids marriage— but one woman's sensual spell clouds his perfect judgment! In *The Millionaire's Convenient Bride* by Catherine George, a dashing millionaire needs a temporary housekeeper—but soon the business arrangement includes a wedding! Finally, in *One-Night Love Child* by Anne McAllister, Flynn doesn't know he's the father of Sara's son—but when he discovers the truth he *will* possess her.... Happy reading from Harlequin Presents!

IN Bed WITH THE Boss

*Chosen by him for business,
taken by him for pleasure...*

A classic collection of office romances by your
favorite authors from Harlequin Presents.

Look out for more, coming soon!

Cathy Williams

TAKEN BY HER GREEK BOSS

In Bed WITH THE Boss

HARLEQUIN®

TORONTO • NEW YORK • LONDON
AMSTERDAM • PARIS • SYDNEY • HAMBURG
STOCKHOLM • ATHENS • TOKYO • MILAN • MADRID
PRAGUE • WARSAW • BUDAPEST • AUCKLAND

ISBN-13: 978-0-373-12711-5
ISBN-10:   0-373-12711-1

TAKEN BY HER GREEK BOSS

First North American Publication 2008.

Copyright © 2007 by Cathy Williams.

All about the author...
Cathy Williams

CATHY WILLIAMS was born in the West Indies
and has been writing Harlequin romances for over
fifteen years. She is a great believer in the power
of perseverance, as she had never written anything
before, and from the starting point of zero has now
fulfilled her ambition to pursue this most enjoyable
of careers. She would encourage any would-be
writer to have faith and go for it!

She lives in the beautiful Warwickshire countryside
with her husband and three children, Charlotte,
Olivia and Emma. When not writing she is hard-
pressed to find a moment's free time in between the
millions of household chores, not to mention being
a one-woman taxi service for her daughters' never-
ending social lives.

She derives inspiration from the hot, lazy, tropical
island of Trinidad (where she was born), from the
peaceful countryside of middle England and, of
course, from her many friends, who are a rich source
of plots and are particularly garrulous when it comes
to describing her heroes. It would seem from their
complaints that tall, dark, and charismatic men are
too few and far between! Her hope is to continue
writing romance fiction and providing those tales of
eternal love for which, she feels, we all strive.

CHAPTER ONE

FOR Nick Papaeliou, the evening was beginning to take on a bizarre, surreal air.

For starters, he was not a man who enjoyed public scenes. He liked to exercise control over every aspect of his life, not least his emotions. And yet, what had happened less than an hour previously? His girlfriend, now relegated to the position of ex-girlfriend, had drunkenly initiated a confrontation that had heralded the demise of their relationship. Of course, he had known for a while that he would have to break off with Susanna, had heard the warning bells begin to ring when her hints had moved from the general arena of *proper relationships* to the more specific one of *wanting to climb off the merry-go-round and settle down before her biological clock began really ticking.* But had he listened? No. The intention to finish with her had hovered on the periphery of his consciousness, but he had been in the middle of a highly complex deal and he had stupidly relegated it to the back-burner.

And then the party tonight. Not just the usual boring model bash to which he had grudgingly agreed to go, knowing that it would be the last with her, but a lavish, private dinner hosted by a fashion-designer couple with a passion for social climbing.

The wine had flowed freely and how true it was that alcohol loosened tongues.

He thought back with distaste to Susanna, the tears, the shouting, the pleading—all conducted in front of an audience of roughly forty people.

Naturally he had left, with every intention of heading back to his penthouse apartment in Mayfair where he would be able to forget the nightmarish previous two hours in front of his laptop computer. It would have been the preferred conclusion to an aberrant evening, but…

He looked sideways at the young woman sitting in the back of the taxi alongside him. Here he was. Waylaid by a fresh-faced blonde who had been waitressing at the party and had coincidentally been leaving at the same time as he had.

He had found himself joining her for a coffee at the café close by and over his cup of strong black coffee, with his defences momentarily lowered after his bruising public bust-up with Susanna, had engaged in the rare pastime of sitting opposite a beautiful woman to whom he was not in the slight-est bit attracted and actually listening to what she had to say, even though much of what she had told him amounted to a story he had heard a thousand times. The beautiful young woman whose dream was to be an actress. Optimism was written all over her youthful face and flowed around him in waves in her excitable conversation and earnest body language.

God, she had made him feel jaded. When he had told her, as kindly and as tactfully as he could, that he was off limits, he had felt, literally, a hundred years old.

How long, he had wondered, could he continue living the bachelor lifestyle? His father had died when he was still a young man in his twenties and his mother had followed him eight years ago. Was that why? Lack of parental pressure to do the expected thing and father the obligatory two point two kids? Or had his single minded and meteoric rise through the ranks provided him with everything wealth and power could buy while, perversely, creating a world into which no one was allowed to take up residence for any period of time?

He honestly didn't know. What he *did* know was that Lily, the part time model who made ends meet however she could while still believing in her dreams, had stirred an unexpectedly almost paternal interest in him.

Which was why, he now contemplated, he was in this taxi with her, having agreed to accompany her back to her place for a nightcap, amused at her palpable horror when he told her that he should really be going back to his place to do a bit of work.

'No one works on a Saturday in the middle of winter at midnight!' she had exclaimed, shocked, and he had almost laughed at her naïveté. She thought, he knew, that she was doing him a good turn in making sure that he had some company after his unpleasant incident at the party, to which she, as everyone else, had been witness. She was also, and he could see this in her wide blue eyes, in awe of him. As most people were. It was something he had become accustomed to taking for granted although, at least in this case, he was pretty sure there was no hidden agenda. She didn't want anything from him and that was refreshing.

The taxi, having wound its way through a myriad deserted streets, all identical in their never-ending rows of unlit terraced houses, finally drew to a stop and, to his further amusement, Lily refused to let him pay, even though she would certainly know him for the billionaire he undoubtedly was.

'It's not much…' she apologised, fumbling in her bag for her front door key.

Nick murmured something suitably polite as she finally

opened the front door, but really she was absolutely spot on. It was a house in an area that might, possibly once, have been considered a fairly decent location, but which the passing years had rendered shabby and depressingly uninviting, and stepping inside only served to cement that first impression.

Nick hadn't been to a place like this for a very long time. He had dragged himself up by his bootlaces, worked like a slave so that he could accumulate the necessary qualifications that would enable him to escape a life of mediocrity in the Home Counties, where his father had eked out a living doing manual work at the Big Houses, as he had liked to call them, the likes of which he would never be able to afford. He had been an uneducated Greek and had never dared to aspire beyond his modest sphere.

Nick had had no intention of following his father's footsteps. A first at university had been the start and followed by a rise through the financial world that had left his peers, most of whom came from a background of Big Houses, gaping and speechless. Now, he no longer worked for anyone. He had his own financial empire and called his own shots. When he opened his mouth, the world listened and paid heed.

And with vast power and wealth had come all the trappings. The place in the sun, rarely visited. The country house that he visited occasionally, whenever the ferocious demands of work allowed him the time off. The chauffeured car, the helicopter for those times when he needed to be somewhere faster than a train or car could take him, the lavish apartment in the heart of one of the most expensive areas in London.

He had long ago left behind the type of place now confronting him, with its tiny handkerchief of a front garden and, even in the forgiving cover of darkness, its signs of disrepair. And here in the small hallway, although much effort had obviously been made to brighten the interior, the cheerful primrose-coloured paint was fighting a losing battle with dodgy woodwork and carpeting that was no longer tired, but downright exhausted.

While Lily bent to unzip her boots, sighing with relief as she yanked the first one off, Nick turned to shut the front door. He was unaware of the sound of footsteps and only realised that there was someone else in the house when he heard Lily give a little yelp.

'Rosie! What are you doing up?'

'Who—' the voice was unusually husky for a woman '—is *that*?'

Nick turned around and found himself staring into a pair of narrowed blue eyes, which were glaring at him. Then he took in the rest of her—small, especially standing next to Lily, and no model's figure, although it was hard to tell because she was swamped in a fairly unflattering ensemble of dressing gown behind which peeked what appeared to be some kind of hideous novelty pyjamas.

'Honestly, Rose, I keep telling you not to wait up for me! I'm a big girl now. I can take care of myself!'

The Rose character, whoever she might be, wore the expression of someone who seriously doubted that statement.

'I have no idea how you can say that, Lily, when you've just waltzed through the door with a complete stranger in tow. At nearly one in the morning. I thought you told me that this was going to be an early one?'

'It *was* early…but…Rose, this is Nick. Nick Papaeliou. Maybe you've heard of him?'

'Of course I haven't heard of him,' Rose snapped. 'You know I don't know a thing about these models you hang around with.'

'Model?' Nick couldn't believe his ears. Nor could he quite believe the way those ferocious blue eyes were scornfully dismissing him. 'You think I'm a model?'

'What else?'

'Oh, Rosie. You have to excuse her, Nick. Rose is very, very protective of me. She thinks I'm going to be gobbled up by a big bad wolf one of these days. But that's cool. Hey, what else do big sisters do?'

'She's your sister?' Nick stared at the small, round woman who was still glaring at him, although he noticed a faint pink colour crawl into her cheeks.

'There's no need to look so stunned,' Rose said coldly.

'We're stepsisters actually,' Lily explained, smiling. 'Isn't it amazing? I mean, you hear so many stories about step-siblings not getting along but Rose and I couldn't be closer if we were proper sisters.' She gave Rose an affectionate squeeze. Even without shoes, she was at least six inches taller. 'Rosie, Nick's just popped by for a nightcap…would you mind? I've got to go to the bathroom.'

Yes, actually, she would mind, but Lily was already vanishing up the stairs, still taking them two at a time, the way she always had even as a kid. Sweet, sunny-natured Lily who thought the best of everyone, even the ones who had Health Hazard written all over their faces. Like this one staring at her, still incredulously digesting the fact that the leggy blonde with the waist-length hair, the one whom he had probably expected to escort home to a suitably empty house, was related to someone who was physically as different from her as chalk from cheese.

Rose stared right back at him. He towered over her and was dangerously good-looking, with a strong, harshly sensual face and black, black hair to match the long black lashes and brooding eyes. It took a lot of will-power not to quail before that singularly unblinking stare. She told herself that he was probably nothing more than a B-grade actor who was accustomed to playing the lead role in hammy TV dramas and didn't know when to drop the act. She didn't know why she had originally assumed he was a model. Definitely not pretty enough.

'So, stepsister Rose, do you always wait up for Lily when she goes out?'

Rose favoured him with a look of haughty disdain. She detected the sarcasm in his voice but she wasn't going to rise to it. She spun round on her heel and headed for the kitchen.

'I'm not going to apologise for being rude, Mr Papaeliou,' she said, the minute they were in the kitchen and he had taken up position on one of the chairs by the pine kitchen table, 'but Lily's been messed around by too many shallow, good-looking men and I'm not going to allow it to happen again…' She must have only just finished making a hot drink for herself because there was no need to boil the kettle. His nightcap, far from being a glass of port or a liqueur, was a mug of coffee handed to him in the manner of someone eager to see him off the premises. She stood in front of him, arms folded. 'She may not think that she needs looking after, and, sure, she's more than capable of running her own life, but when it comes to emotions my sister can be very trusting. She doesn't need to get involved with a two-bit actor on the make.'

Nick, for the first time in his life, felt himself struggling to get a handle on the situation.

'Two bit actor?'

'What else? You might play the action hero in whatever third-rate movies you've been in, but you can drop the macho act. It doesn't wash with me. All I know is that Lily is a sucker when it comes to a good-looking man with a few chat-up lines, but they never stay the course and she's had her heart broken too many times…'

Two-bit actor? Action hero? The woman had the bare-faced audacity to make him sound like a comic-book character! But he was certainly not going to allow himself to be dragged into a stand-up fight with a woman with the personality of a Rottweiler. 'Hence you're her self-appointed watchdog. That's very noble of you,' Nick said coolly. 'Does Lily appreciate your over-zealous concern? Or do you save these little speeches for when her back's turned?' He placed the mug on the table without drinking any of the coffee. 'I hate to burst your bubble, but I'm not an empty-headed male model out to sleep with the nearest attractive woman, nor am I a two bit actor with an identity problem.'

'No? Well, it doesn't matter. Model, actor…creative director with an empty casting couch…it's all much of a muchness. Lily's just emerged from a relationship that ended badly and I'm making sure that she doesn't get taken in by another man with too much looks and too few scruples for his own good. I wish there were a more polite way of warning you off, but there isn't.'

Nick was accustomed to women pandering to him, hanging onto his every word, courting him with their feminine wiles. Could his night go any more off course? From a showdown that, inevitably, would reach the gossip pages in some rag, to a confrontation with a perfect stranger who was either partially unhinged or just too plain bloody outspoken for her own good.

Before he could reply to that blazing, generalised condemnation, Lily burst into the kitchen, apologising profusely and winningly for taking so long, but she'd just had to have a quick shower because she'd felt hideously grubby and knew, just knew that she'd stunk of cigarette smoke because everybody, but everybody there had been smoking and not all of it the run-of-the-mill tobacco.

Even in the early hours of the morning and after a long day doing a tiring job, she still managed to look incredibly fresh and vital and hopelessly young. It was ludicrous that her sister could imply that he, Nick Papaeliou, who could have any woman he wanted, would be attracted to Lily.

'Have you two been getting to know one another?' Lily asked brightly and Nick, looking at Rose from under his lashes, saw her glance with muted antagonism at him. Lily helped herself to some water from the tap and then turned around and perched against the counter so that she could look at them both.

'Oh, absolutely,' Nick drawled smoothly, giving Rose a slow, meaningful smile. 'Like a house on fire…'

'Oh, great!' She turned to Rose. 'Poor Nick broke up with his girlfriend tonight and it's always nice to be in company when you're down in the dumps.'

The meaningful smile slowly disappeared as Rose raised her eyebrows and nodded her head slowly.

'I was far from down in the dumps, Lily.' He tried to smile that one off, but he was irritably conscious of her sister's eyes fastened on his face. 'In fact, our relationship was on its way out. Susanna only did what I myself would have done the following day.' How was he now having an inappropriately private conversation with two women he had never seen in his life before tonight?

'Why would you go to a party with someone you wanted to ditch?' Rose asked innocently and Nick gritted his teeth together. 'I mean, the poor woman probably thought that you really cared about her.'

'If you knew Susanna, the very last word you would use to describe her would be poor.'

'Still…' Rose allowed that one little word to drop into the silence.

Looking at her, Nick momentarily forgot Lily's presence. 'Still…what?'

'Must be awful to break up with someone you care about in front of other people. I always think that when I open the newspapers and they're full of some poor celebrity couple who end up being forced to wash all their dirty linen in public. And in a way, that's not even as bad as the dirty linen being washed in front of friends…she must have been feeling pretty desperate…'

Lily was watching this interchange with a certain amount of bewilderment.

'And on that note…' Nick stood up. Surprisingly, exchanging barbs with Rose had so completely absorbed his attention that nothing else had occupied his mind. Not Susanna, not work, and he had completely forgotten Lily's presence even though she had been standing in his direct line of vision.

'Oh, dear…leaving so soon? Well, shall I call a cab for you? You won't find one here, you know. It's not central enough. Lily…' Rose looked at her sister '…you look done in. Why don't you hit the sack and I'll wait up until Nick leaves?'

'Don't be silly, Rose.' She yawned widely. 'How can I invite Nick here for a nightcap and then disappear off to bed?'

'*I* have already given him a nightcap. It was called a cup of coffee.'

'Rose doesn't do an awful lot of drinking…' Lily smiled at Nick '…do you, Rosie?'

'I'm sure Mr Papaeliou isn't interested in my alcohol consumption.' Lord, but she sounded prim and proper.

'The name's Nick,' Nick said irritably.

Rose ignored him. 'There. You're falling asleep on your feet, Lily. Go to bed. I'll see Mr Pa…*Nick*…out.'

'Well…'

'I can lie in in the morning,' Rose insisted. 'You know you always go to the gym first thing.'

'S'pose…'

Rose guided her sister in the direction of the staircase so that the temptation of bed was just a little more irresistible. 'Well nothing. You've been on your feet for the better part of the day while I've been here, just lolling around and taking it easy.'

'If you're sure…'

Oh, boy, Rose was absolutely sure. She gave Nick a gimlet-eyed stare, but as soon as Lily had vanished up the stairs he removed his jacket and lounged against the wall, looking at her.

Rose, all at once and unbidden, became acutely conscious of her inappropriate garb. Something about the subdued lighting in the hall, the knowledge that Lily was upstairs, probably about to crawl into bed, the way he was looking at her in that perfectly still way… She tightened her dressing gown around her and clung onto her virtuous sense of authority. Revealing even a glimpse of her nightwear, namely pyjamas patterned with prancing reindeer, which had been given to her as a Christmas present by a friend who specialised in silly gifts, would undermine everything she now wanted to convey.

'Don't tell me,' he said, moving towards her, which, for some reason, she found horribly disconcerting, 'you're about to resume your attack, having frogmarched Lily to bed.'

'I did *not* frogmarch her.'

'As good as. So come on, then, let's call a taxi and get it over and done with.' He followed her into the kitchen, watched as she sat down and scrolled through the address book on her mobile phone, then made the call. While she did, she looked at Nick and tried not to let his presence overwhelm her,

because even after such a brief spell in his company she knew,
could just sense, that he was the sort of man who could inspire
abject fear should he want to. Not exactly a people person,
she thought nastily. The sort of man who picked up women
and dropped them without a backward glance or a twinge of
guilt. Like the poor Susanna who had been fired up enough
to make a fool of herself in front of her friends.

They had fifteen minutes to talk and Rose wasn't going to
waste a single one of those minutes, but before she could utter
a word Nick strolled towards her, cornering her in her chair so
that she could feel the full, undiluted power of his personality.

'But before you say anything, I think it's my turn, don't
you?' He smiled.

Rose refused to be intimidated. Just who did he think he
was anyway? She made herself breathe evenly. Up close like
this, his eyes were the deepest of greens, the colour of the fathomless sea. Right now the fathomless sea was revealing some
very icy depths.

'I think you should get a life,' Nick said grimly, 'and let
your sister lead her own. Is it natural for you to wait up for
her like a mother hen? Making sure she gets home safe and
sound? You may think it natural. I, on the other hand, consider
it sad, as would most people.' He couldn't believe he was
having this conversation. Did he care what this woman
thought of him? Did he care what anyone thought of him?
True freedom, he had always thought, was the freedom from
caring about other people's opinions. So why the hell was a
pair of defiant blue eyes making him want to justify himself?

Rose blushed and for a few seconds was lost for words.
Somewhere at the back of her mind, she knew that he was
making sense, but looking out for Lily was a habit born of
time and one that she couldn't seem to let go. Their parents,

her mother and stepfather, had died when they were still very young and they had gone to live with their aunt and uncle who were, as they were fond of saying, travellers in search of the meaning of life. Rose had discovered that this basically meant that they moved from pillar to post at a whim, with the practical concerns of two young people being only a minor technical hitch.

Nearly seven years older than her stepsister, Rose had been the sensible one who had made sure that Lily had someone grounded to whom she could turn and so, from the age of ten, she had become accustomed to looking out for her sister. But now Lily was twenty-two. Did she really still need the sensible older sister to wait up for her?

'I don't care what you think.'

'What do you think your sister would say if she knew that you were warning me away?'

'I think she would see it for the loving gesture that it is.'

'Or maybe she might see it as an infringement of her right to lead her life the way she sees fit.'

'Who are you,' Rose spluttered, 'to tell me what I should and shouldn't do?'

'Well, not a male model nor an actor, nor, for that matter, a seedy film director with an empty casting couch.' He moved away from her chair and sat down, but pulling the kitchen chair close to hers so that there was no escaping his stifling presence. Where was he going with this particular piece of justification? he wondered.

'I don't care what job you do, Mr Papaeliou...'

'I'm in finance, as a matter of fact. And believe me, when it comes to women, I don't need to entice them with an empty casting couch.'

'Whatever you do doesn't change the fact that you're a man

who can break up traumatically with a woman, look around you, and within minutes be on the trail of another notch for your bedpost.'

Nick was enraged. Never had he been the object of such an unprecedented attack by someone who didn't know him. Without vanity or pride, he could say that people tiptoed around him, the only exceptions being women at the end of a relationship who could, like Susanna, become hysterical and accusatory, but that was something he had always easily dealt with because, and his conscience was utterly clear on this point, he never made the mistake of making promises he would later fail to keep. He never spoke of love or allowed ideas of permanence and commitment to blur the edges of a relationship. He was speechless now at her sweeping assumptions, but absolutely through with defending himself and he stood up and began walking out of the kitchen while Rose gathered herself and followed him.

She had exhausted her argument and now there was nothing left to be said. Nick obviously thought the same thing because he stuck on his coat in silence, only looking at her when he was about to leave, with his hand on the door knob, in fact.

Rose pulled her dressing gown even tighter around her. In the half light, the man was frighteningly sexy and she felt an unwelcome shiver race down her spine, like the light, trailing touch of a finger. No, he certainly wouldn't need an empty casting couch to attract women, she thought. He just had to look at them. She harnessed her thoughts back to her sister and primly congratulated herself on spotting a heartbreaker and trying to do something about it.

'Thanks for the coffee,' he said coldly, 'and the warning. Take a tip from me—get a life, spend your Saturdays doing something and then maybe you wouldn't work yourself up into a lather over your sister and what she's getting up to. I'll wait outside for the cab.'

With that he opened the door and, with perfect timing, the taxi pulled up.

Infuriated and insulted he might be, but Nick was hardly aware of the drive back to his house. There was a message on his answering machine. He played it back to discover that it was from Susanna, apologising in a trembling voice. He erased it without bothering to hear it fully out.

Damned Rose! Lurching out of nowhere like a furious little avenging angel, and now he couldn't erase her from his mind. Experienced as Nick was in compartmentalising his personal life, he was sourly aware that the abrasive woman had rubbed him the wrong way to such an extent that he spent the better part of what remained of the night brooding and not even thoughts of work were sufficiently tantalising a distraction.

The furious avenging angel, less furious now as she lay in bed some twenty minutes after she had slammed the front door behind him, stared up at the ceiling and glumly admitted to herself that the man had got under her skin. *Get a life.* The taunt rankled because it had hit its target with the unswerving accuracy of a guided missile. Twenty-nine years old, as good as, and here she was, wearing ridiculous pyjamas and still playing caretaker to a sister who no longer needed caretaking.

Where had all the party times gone? Had there been any? Tony and Flora, as her aunt and uncle had insisted they be called, had done everything to encourage a wild and carefree lifestyle. Life, she had been told so often that she knew the script off by heart, was a wonderful and exciting place to be approached with curiosity and zest. Education was fine within reason, but the greater education was the *Education of Life,* which could loosely be translated into *The Lifestyle of a Nomad*. It had suited Tony and Flora but to Rose it spelt sickening upheavals and she had fought a rearguard action through her quiet rebellions. She had developed an aversion to pulses and soya and had insisted on burgers and fries, had immersed herself in her books, studying until her aunt and uncle had finally stopped telling her to go out and have some fun, had refused to wear the gypsy skirts and patchwork coats garnered from Oxfam shops, more through a healthy sense of self-preservation than personal dislike, and had made sure that Lily was as grounded as it was possible for her to be considering their weird lifestyle.

And in between all that, the parties had never happened and by the time Tony and Flora had zoomed off in their camper van, headed for the Cornish coast, where they still now lived, the ability to abandon herself to the freedom of youth had slipped past her. She had gone to university, worked hard and set her sights on achieving everything that she felt she had lacked in her formative years. Security.

Very important. For her. And for Lily. Even if Lily gave no thought to it. With the sort of lifestyle that she led, doing jobs off and on, trying out for parts in plays or commercials, most of which she never got, she needed at least one area in her life upon which she could rely and, having seen her sister on her roller-coaster rides with unsuitable men, Rose was determined to make sure that she at least provided Lily with a core of emotional stability in her chaotic world.

Of course, rushing in with dire words of warning the day after wasn't going to work, so Rose prudently decided to leave the matter alone for a while and then, on one of the rare nights when they were both in and sharing a bowl of pasta without Lily having to rush off or Rose having to work late, she said, tentatively, 'Seen anything more of that guy…can't quite remember his name…the one who brought you back after that party a couple of weeks ago…?'

Lily, twirling some spaghetti round her fork, looked at Rose and grinned. 'You mean Nick, Nick Papaeliou…how on earth could you have forgotten his name, Rosie? I don't think anyone's ever forgotten his name before. I've seen him twice, actually.'

Rose spluttered on a mouthful of pasta and cleared her throat with some water. 'Twice! That's twice more than I thought you had, considering you never mentioned a word to me.'

'I meant to tell you, Rosie, but…'

'But what?' she asked casually, thinking of that dark, cynical face and stabbing an errant mushroom with her fork. She was reading guilt in the way her sister's eyes shifted away from her.

'I just thought you might give me a hard time. Nick got the impression that you didn't much care for him.'

'Me?' Rose laughed carelessly. 'Rubbish—the man's obviously paranoid.'

'Oh, Nick wouldn't be paranoid about anything, Rosie. I mean…he's got everything anyone could ever want or need. Apparently you thought that he was a two-bit actor.' Lily giggled. 'Wish I could have been a fly on the wall to have seen his expression when you said that. He looked outraged even when he repeated it to me.'

'I admit I may have mistaken him for someone in the acting profession,' Rose said carefully. 'I don't mean to sound the alarm bells unnecessarily, Lily, but he didn't strike me as the most reliable man in town.'

'What do you mean—"reliable"?'

'Oh, the steady-as-a-rock kind. I just think that it's so easy to be impressed by someone for all the wrong reasons.

They may be good looking or rich…and in fact they could just be bad news.'

'And I do have a history of going with the wrong guys,' Lily admitted ruefully, which was Rose's cue to breathe a sigh of relief and nod her head in vigorous agreement. 'But you're quite mistaken about Nick, Rosie. Honestly, I'm not impressed by how he looks or what he has…he's just a very nice guy.'

Nice? Nice? Were they talking about the same human being?

Then it occurred to her that he probably was a very nice man to Lily. A stunning face and a sexy body probably turned him into a very nice man indeed. On the other hand, he had had no reason to be nice to her and so had shown his true colours. He could give lessons on arrogance if her sister only but knew.

'If you got to know him a little bit better, then you would agree with me, you really would. In fact…'

'Um?'

'Well, I *was* going to actually mention this to you later…but…and this is the sort of guy he is, really cool…he's invited both of us to a bit of a bash next Saturday. Even though you called him a two bit actor…' another mini fit of giggles giving Rose a breather in which to digest this bolt from the blue '…he still stressed that he wanted us both to go along. Isn't that sweet? We'll have to go shopping. Apparently he's having something small at a very exclusive club he owns…anybody who's anybody's going to be there. And us! How exciting is that?'

'Not very,' Rose said, panicked. 'I mean…I'm not sure at all…I don't think…' Just the thought of something small at a very exclusive club owned by Nick Papaeliou was enough to bring her out in a cold sweat.

'I won't let you just write him off without a second chance,

Rosie.' Then Lily pulled out the most ancient emotional trump card in the deck. 'If you really cared about me the way you say you do, then you'll come…'

CHAPTER TWO

NICK HELPED HIMSELF to another drink. He felt restless. The party that had been arranged specifically for the benefit of Lily, though that was something she would never know, was in full swing. He had asked all the movers and shakers in the world of theatre, teased their palates by throwing in a few big names in business, the sort of men and women who were interested in promoting the Arts and were willing to put their money where their mouth was, and the supermodels were really the icing on the cake.

Not a single person had declined the invitation, even though it was very much a last-minute affair. Parties thrown by him were few and far between and had enough cachet to attract even the most sought-after celebrities.

Unfortunately, the belle of the ball, so to speak, had still not arrived. Nor had her sister.

Nick's gaze strayed once more to the door and he looked at his watch. It didn't take a genius to work out why they were late. Rose had either decided not to come or else had employed delaying tactics. It would have been a hell of a lot easier if he had not asked her along, but his memory of their last encounter had preyed on his mind and eventually he had worked out that inviting her, letting her see for herself how little he needed to pursue a woman because of her looks, would even out the score. She had dismissed him and Nick Papaeliou didn't like being dismissed. He particularly didn't like being dismissed for the wrong reasons.

He was still staring at the door when it opened. He saw Lily first, exquisite in a pale blue dress that was very simple, just a short silky shift with a very respectable round collar, saw her look round the room, searching him out, and he found himself trying to stare behind her to see whether Rose had come or not.

He finished his drink and headed towards them and as he neared them he saw her, half ducking behind the door.

'You're here.' A warm smile for Lily and then he stepped around her to where Rose was nervously hovering just out of sight of the crowd. 'And so are you. I'm surprised. I thought you might decide that this wasn't the sort of thing you were interested in attending.'

How right he was. Over four days, Rose had made several futile attempts to wriggle out of her sister's rash promise that they would both be overjoyed to attend whatever posh party Nick had arranged. She had valiantly plugged the Nothing To Wear excuse, which had been overruled before it had even had time to gain the necessary momentum, then had come a pious, self-sacrificing But I Wouldn't Want To Get In Your Way, and when that had fallen on deaf ears she had resorted to the truth, which was that she was totally uninterested in those sorts of things, big parties full of people talking at one another and peering around to see if somebody more interesting happened to be lurking on the horizon.

The truth was that she didn't want to see Nick. She disapproved of his involvement with her sister and she bitterly resented his arrogant, insulting response to her perfectly reasonable request that he take his attentions elsewhere.

Now, as she looked at him, she felt all that resentment gathering pace, like a snowball turning into an avalanche.

He looked magnificent. White shirt, black trousers, but instead of looking conventional he looked darkly, broodingly, raffishly sexy. Something about the way he had rolled the sleeves to his elbows. Or maybe it was his colouring that did it.

Rose shuffled away from the comforting wall that separated her from the rest of the crowd inside and tried not to scowl.

'It isn't,' she said shortly.

'Well, don't hide away out here, you two. Come inside and meet all the beautiful people.' Okay, he knew that that would probably send her nervous system into furious overdrive, but he couldn't help himself.

Lily, of course, responded with predictable enthusiasm, happily taking the arm he offered, while her sister looked at his other arm, also being proffered, and ignored it.

She felt awkward enough in her outfit without having to suffer the indignity of everyone looking at them, puzzling out who the short, dumpy woman in the black dress was. Lily might hang off his arm and look as though that was her rightful place. Rose, on the other hand, knew that were she to hang off his other arm the effect would be just the opposite. So she walked a little distance apart, grateful that Lily was keeping up the conversation with her bubbly chatter.

'I'll get you two a drink, shall I?'

'Ooh. A glass of champagne would be great, Nick.' Lily's eyes were everywhere, like a kid in a toy shop.

'And for you?'

Rose met his amused eyes steadily. 'I'm fine just at the moment.'

'No, you're not. I'll get you a glass of wine. It'll help you to relax.'

'I'm perfectly relaxed,' Rose lied, and he grinned broadly at her.

'In that case, you're giving an excellent imitation of someone who would rather be anywhere else in the world but here.'

He disappeared, feeling suddenly invigorated. He had never prided himself on his altruism. Sure, he gave massive donations of money to charity, but all of that he left to his financial department. In the case of Lily, he was doing a good deed for which he would get nothing in return. Except her gratitude, most probably, although gratitude was something he never requested from anyone and rarely appreciated. Yes, indeed, being Mr Good Guy was proving to be a very enjoyable novelty.

Of course, he mused, a little gratitude from her sister might be pretty satisfying.

He caught himself scanning the room, making sure that Rose was where he had left her and, sure enough, she was, although Lily was beginning to look a little edgy. By the time he made it back to Rose, it was to find her standing on her own.

'Lily's disappeared,' she greeted him.

'So I see.'

'She recognised some people from her last stint in the theatre.'

'Rude of her not to introduce you to them.'

'I…I told her to go ahead.' Rose looked at him defiantly. 'It's important that she tries to make a few connections. Apparently, that's how it works in the acting business. You can't come to a do like this and huddle on the sidelines.' She accepted her glass of wine while he deposited the unwanted champagne on one of the many handy chest-height tables that dotted the room. Tall bar stools were positioned by some of the tables, but most of these were unused. Rose supposed that sitting down wasn't conducive enough to mingling.

'No. It's all about networking,' Nick agreed.

'And I really don't want to keep you from that.'

'I have no need to network.' He shrugged. 'There's nothing I need from anyone here. They are my guests and a good time will be had by all because they offer each other opportunities. The people in the acting profession will be networking with the businessmen who make their world tick financially, the businessmen will be lusting after the models, the models will be intrigued by the celebrities—'

'And you will observe them all.'

Nick returned his gaze to her face, which was cool and assessing. He frowned.

'What's wrong with that?'

'You're like a scientist looking at the rest of the world through a microscope, examining interesting little bugs.'

'You know,' he drawled, 'maybe I shouldn't let you loose in the room, not with that knack you have of rubbing people up the wrong way.'

Rose flushed. 'I didn't realise that I was rubbing you up the wrong way. I was just making an observation.'

'The only way to succeed in life is to develop the ability to read other people.' He looked at her carefully and realised that he was intrigued by her personality, proving yet again to himself that he needed a little novelty in his life. First Lily and now her sister. Making money was predictable. Closing deals brought an adrenaline rush, yes, but it was something that was over quickly. And women…hardly any surprises there. Until now. He decided that he would spend a few more minutes with her, sparing her the trauma of mixing, in other words doing her a good deed.

'Oh, yes?' she enquired politely and he frowned at her, unimpressed with that hint of mild boredom in her voice.

'Take yourself, for example.' Oh, yes, that did the trick. He could almost see her begin to bristle. 'Here you are, hating every minute of this party, dragged along by Lily who, in her own sweet way, is as stubborn as a mule—'

'I'm not sure where you're going with this. I've already told you that this isn't my sort of thing—'

'And you would love to put yourself firmly above everyone here, but I'll just bet you feel awkward and gauche. Am I right?' Since when did a woman find his company boring? It was inconceivable.

'No. No, I don't...' She should never have worn this black, shapeless dress. Tall, skinny people could pull off shapeless because everyone would know that, underneath, they had rangy, slender bodies. And, yes, she did feel awkward and gauche, but there was no need to have the fact pointed out to her. 'Anyway, why did you ask me along if you knew that I wasn't going to enjoy myself? If you're such a brilliant reader of people, you must have known that I wouldn't fit in with this crowd.'

'It's always good to face your fears.'

'Oh, so you are doing me a favour, in other words.'

'And I notice you aren't suitably grateful.'

Rose downed the remainder of her wine and snorted in an appropriately unfeminine way. She picked up the champagne that he had left on the table and swallowed a mouthful, drawing in her breath as the bubbles went down. The little glittery black bag that she had borrowed from Lily, and which she was clutching in her left hand, seemed a ridiculous accessory. Her skin crawled at the thought that he was laughing at her, finding her awkward and gauche. The champagne seemed to be finished and she seriously contemplated another drink.

'I'm going to have to circulate now.'

'Don't let me stand in your way.'

'Oh, but you are,' Nick drawled smoothly. Two glasses on the trot had brought a pink flush to her cheeks. 'I'm running this show and it's my duty to make sure that no one is left standing next to the wall on their own, quietly drinking themselves into a stupor.'

Rose felt the colour crawl into her face as her role loomed before her in all its unmistakable hideousness. She was Lily's chaperone and her host's burden. He would fob her off on one of his guests or else deliver her back to her sister because he thought that if he didn't, she would end up making a fool of herself. Mortification replaced the light headed sensation induced by the wine and champagne and brought her crashing back down to the reality crowding around her.

'I'm not going to drink myself into a stupor,' she snapped. 'You needn't worry that I'm going to embarrass you in front of your glittering guests.'

'Embarrass me?'

'By drinking too much and falling into a heap on the floor.'

'Why would I be embarrassed if you make a spectacle of yourself?' He sighed impatiently and led her to one of the bar stools at the table closest to them. The woman was difficult and tactless and of course he shouldn't concern himself with her, but he felt an irrational need to take her under his wing. Because, he told himself, she was Lily's sister and while *he* might not be embarrassed if Rose got drunk and made a fool of herself, her sister almost certainly would. So, gentleman that he was, he would forgo his duty to circulate and spend a little time with her instead. No hardship. The crowd seemed to be doing splendidly without his input. The wonders of limitless alcohol, he thought. And of course the seduction of preening and strutting in front of people who counted. He had been keeping a watchful eye on Lily. Next to some of the more seasoned networkers, she was holding her own and drinking, he noticed, remarkably little. A wise head on young shoulders.

'I thought you were going to mingle with your guests,' Rose said, then, as if giving things a second thought, she sighed into the glass of orange juice that had mysteriously appeared in front of her. 'I'm not being a particularly nice person, am I?'

Nick shook his head, relaxing and slinging one arm over the slatted back of his bar stool.

'Well, nor are you!'

He smiled and raised his eyebrows. 'That's the worst apology I've ever heard.'

'It wasn't meant to be an apology.'

'Oh. You mean you were just making an observation about yourself.'

Rose decided to change the subject altogether. When he looked at her she felt simultaneously incredibly self-conscious, which was maddening, and resentful of him for making her feel that way.

'It's a very nice place you have here.'

'Oh, don't tell me you're going to go all polite on me now.' This happening party of his seemed to be a long way away.

'How on earth did you make so much money?'

'Ah. That's more like it. Crashing through those flimsy barriers called tact and really speaking your mind without bothering to gift-wrap anything.'

'You *did* tell me not to be polite.' Rose, who was not accustomed to flirting, was uneasily aware of a certain undercurrent between them that was thrilling and frightening at the same time. As were those amazing eyes of his, resting thoughtfully on her face. She knew that she was just being stupid but her heart was thudding inside her like a hammer and everything, all her senses, seemed heightened, stretched taut like a piece of elastic.

'So…?' she persisted.

'Worked my way up.' Nick nodded to one of the waiters who were invisibly collecting empty glasses and asked him for a whisky and soda.

'Up from where?'

'This is really a very boring story.'

'You mean you don't like other people observing you under their microscope even though you enjoy observing *them* under yours.'

Meaning that personal confidences were not part of his routine when it came to women. However, his history was no secret. Anyone could access its bare bones from the thousands of entries to be found on him on the Internet. Where was the harm in saving her the bother of looking him up, if her curiosity got the better of her?

'A simple tale of a Greek immigrant who fell in love with an English beauty,' he said casually. Did anyone know how his parents had sustained him? Had faith in him? 'They worked all the hours God made to make ends meet and to put me through private school.' Well, that was no big confidence. It was there in his profile somewhere.

'That's wonderful.'

'Is it?'

'Of course it is.' She rather thought that he would have done just fine whatever school he had attended, but, compared to her background, it must have been marvellous to have had parents who would have been willing to do whatever it took for their child to pursue a proper education.

'Where are they now?'

'No more. They both died a long time ago.' He looked away, annoyed because this was all in the past and why the hell was he talking about it anyway?

'I'm sorry.'

'And I do need to actually mingle with the people I have invited here.' He stood up and looked down at her. 'I can introduce you or I can leave you here on your own. Take your pick.'

So that brief truce between them was over. Rose was quietly relieved. Just then, she had felt something sneak up on her, something unwanted that had made her feel giddy and out of control.

'I'm fine,' she told him with a distant smile. 'You go mix. I'll have a hunt around for Lily. Sorry for having taken up too much of your valuable time.' When it came to sarcasm, she was as good as him any day.

Anyway, it was much easier now. Nearly everyone there was mellower by a fair few glasses of champagne. They barely noticed her skirting through them. In fact, Rose felt virtually invisible.

She found Lily in the middle of a small group of men, not saying much but paying a lot of attention, and very sober. That was good. For Rose, she would leave this evening behind and return to her normal life. For Lily, this was a chance to meet people, to get her face known and, for her sake, Rose hoped that the evening would turn out to be a success.

She hovered briefly on the fringe, then wandered through the crowd and, after a couple more glasses of wine, found that chatting to them wasn't the nightmare she had predicted. Somewhere Nick was lurking, although she couldn't actually see him anywhere.

Like Cinderella, she was ready to leave by the stroke of midnight. She seemed to be in a minority of one. The drink was still flowing, her sister was absorbed talking to a couple of guys, her face fresh and animated, and Rose had had enough. She had listened to people talk about other people, had eavesdropped boring conversations about scripts that had never got off the ground and arguments with directors who didn't know what they were talking about and lottery grants that should have gone to art projects but had ended up going to crazy organisations that wasted the money and went bankrupt within two years. She had eaten the most amazing finger food she had ever tasted, served by the most attentive staff she had ever seen, and refused enough glasses of wine or champagne to fill a cellar.

After fifteen minutes of trying to attract Lily's attention, Rose gave up and headed out of the room in search of a breath of fresh air.

Outside was a corridor that circled the club area and off which, like little nodules from a main stem, were rooms behind which were probably offices, although Rose couldn't tell because the doors were all shut. The floors were pale cream marble, merging into the pale cream marble of the walls, along which hung abstract paintings that looked particularly unappealing in the subdued lighting.

She drifted along, deciding to give her sister precisely half an hour more networking time before dragging her out of the place, and was about to head back when she spotted the light from under the door. It was just a narrow strip, but in the relative darkness of the corridor as bright as a beacon and she didn't hesitate. She walked right towards it and pushed open the door. She hadn't known what to expect but she certainly hadn't expected to find Nick there, installed in front of his computer and surrounded by all the paraphernalia of a home office.

'Sorry,' she mumbled, backing out, but he had already

pushed his chair away from the desk and was pinning her in her tracks just by looking at her. A further, more elaborate apology formed somewhere in her mind but didn't quite manage to connect with her vocal cords, which seemed to have seized up.

In the intervening silence, he propped his feet up on his desk and relaxed back, hands folded behind his head.

'Looking for something?' His dark eyebrows rose in amused enquiry and Rose cleared her throat.

'No. I just happened to be…'

'Escaping all the fun and laughter? Come in and close the door behind you.' He paused. 'Well? I don't bite. At least, not unless I'm invited to.'

Rose, calm, efficient, always-in-control Rose, was beginning to feel very addled. Of course, she ought to graciously thank him for inviting her to his private function, politely turn down his offer to step inside, which had the vaguely dangerous undertones of what the spider had said to the fly, and hunt down Lily pronto.

She found herself obeying him, however, and shutting the door behind her, although once she had done so her legs refused to cooperate by propelling her towards the chair that he was now indicating.

'Sit.'

'I…I'm really on my way out, actually.' Vocal cords found. Thank heavens! 'I came outside to get a breath of fresh air and saw…well, the light under the door. What on earth are you doing?' This was much better. Her brain was beginning to function. She made it to the chair and sat down.

'What does it look like I'm doing?'

'Isn't it a bit rude for the host to be working at his own party?'

'I think everyone can manage fine without me for half an

hour.' Nick shrugged and continued to look at her, his expression unreadable. She looked awkward in her dress, as if wearing dresses was not something that came naturally to her but having found herself cornered into buying one, she had opted for the least flattering. Every single woman at the party had made a very special effort to wear something that would make them stand out in the crowd. Rose, on the other hand, had worn something that shrieked *background*. Briefly, Nick wondered what she would look like underneath the shapeless black garment and drew his breath in sharply, surprised at the thought.

'Besides, there was no choice. I had an urgent phone call from Australia requesting some information to be emailed to them.'

'Do you ever stop working?'

'Occasionally.' He lowered his eyes. Something about the shape of her breasts, just discernible under the dress, was kick-starting his imagination. 'Lily seems to be enjoying herself.'

'Yes. Yes, she does.'

'But I guess you probably found the whole thing a little…boring…'

She shrugged. 'Not at all,' she told him politely.

'You looked bored every time I saw you.'

'You were watching me?'

Nick didn't like the intonation in her voice when she said that. 'It's my duty to make sure that my guests are having a good time.'

'Then I'm surprised your keen sense of duty allowed you to sneak off to this office and work.' Yet again, she had the nagging, unpleasant suspicion that she was a charity case. 'Anyway, it was very interesting. It always is, meeting people from different walks of life.'

'Now why do I get the feeling that you don't really mean that?' When she didn't answer, he added, interested against his will, 'What's *your* walk of life?'

'I beg your pardon?'

'What do you do for a living?'

'I…I work in computers.' God, that sounded dull, especially when she considered the flamboyant, beautiful people who cluttered his life. How on earth, as a businessman, was he so well connected with the media set? she wondered. Then the question was answered virtually before it was posed. He dated cover girls. Money and looks would always be attracted to money and looks.

'That's very interesting.'

'There's no need to patronise me.'

'I'm not. What exactly do you do? In computers?'

'Nothing very exciting.'

At this point, Nick knew that he should just give up. Getting anything out of this woman was about as rewarding and straightforward as pulling teeth, and if it was one thing he didn't do, it was to work at making small talk with a woman. But her awkward response was like an invitation to press harder. In front of him, the screensaver came up on the computer and he switched it off.

'What does that mean?'

'Look—' Rose looked at him steadily '—I know you probably feel sorry for me…'

'Why should I feel sorry for you?'

'Because I don't slot into your category of an interesting woman.'

'As you quite rightly pointed out, it's always an eye opener meeting people from different walks of life.'

'Well, if you really want to know, I pretty much do everything with computers. Programming, updating systems, designing websites…' She heard herself rattling off a curriculum vitae that sounded deadly dull. 'It's actually very absorbing,' she stressed.

'I'm sure it is,' Nick agreed. 'Odd that you and your sister should have ended up in such completely different worlds. Computing and acting…'

Rose shrugged and stood up. 'I've got to go and find Lily. It's late. Time to head back.'

Nick met his fair share of clever, career-oriented women in his working life. He had frequently sat opposite top female lawyers in the early hours of the morning closing deals. Several of them had even tried to flirt with him, but he had never been interested in developing a relationship with any of them outside the boardroom. Put simply, nothing could compete with the archetypal brainless bimbo when it came to relaxation. Who needed to be mentally challenged twenty four seven? He had derived enough mental challenges in his working life.

Or so he had always maintained.

Right now, he was beginning to feel inordinately curious about what the computer whiz kid did in her spare time.

'Is this a late night for you?' he asked blandly.

Rose was suitably riled by the question. 'Not particularly,' she lied. 'But there's a limit to how long I can carry on chatting to people I don't know about things I'm not particularly interested in.'

'What would you rather be doing?'

'Going to bed, as a matter of fact.'

'With anyone in particular?'

Rose's mouth dropped open at the sheer audacity of the question, which had sprung from nothing but, once voiced, seemed to fill the room with thick, electric tension.

'I really don't think that's any of your business,' she finally managed to stutter, red-faced. She turned and began walking towards the door, head held high. He might be a millionaire many times over, but that didn't give him the right to say whatever he wanted to say and ask whatever he wanted to ask, without reserve.

She was aware of him behind her before she had even reached the door and when he stood in front of her, blocking her exit, she had to clench her hands at her sides to steady her nerves.

'I like things that aren't my business,' Nick murmured lazily. 'So tell me what you do in your spare time. When you go out until the early hours of the morning.'

He towered over her and she felt as if she were suffocating. Was he laughing at her? She rather imagined that he was because he certainly wasn't interested in anything she had to say. He was bored with his own party and had decided to have a little fun at her expense. She was sure of it.

Having worked all that out, it still left her with the little problem of how to get out of the room when he was standing in front of the door like a prison warden with a taste for sadism.

The man was loathsome. Yes, he was sinfully good-looking and, yes, she could see those flashes of charm that turned women into mindless robots ready to do whatever he asked them to do, but to her he was someone who was happy to play with other people, in much the same way as a cat played with a mouse. No serious harm intended, just a spot of good fun.

'I don't have to do anything,' Rose told him coolly. 'Lily's always been the clubber.'

'And you've always been…what?' Hand it to her, he thought, she wasn't going to let herself be daunted by him, even though her mounting colour signalled her discomfort. Nor was she flattered by his interest. In fact, he would have been hard-pressed to think of any woman less flattered by his undivided attention. That in itself was an interesting concept.

'I talk when I go out with my friends,' Rose said quietly.

'And I don't need to drink to excess or have loud music blaring in the background to feel as though I'm having a good time.'

Nick could hear the implicit sarcasm in her voice and was amused by it.

'Sounds like fun.'

'Yes. Yes, it is.'

'And what do you do afterwards?'

'What do you mean?'

'When you've had fun setting the world to rights?'

'I don't set the world to rights.' Rose gritted her teeth together and reminded herself that he was just goading her and that the last thing she should do was play into his hands by reacting. 'And even if we did sit around setting the world to rights, it would still be a heck of a lot more fun than slowly getting drunk and bitching about everyone and everything.'

'Referring to anyone in particular?'

'Several in general,' she said waspishly, 'and they're all out there. I believe they're called your friends.'

If she had hoped to insult him, then she had been mistaken, because instead of being suitably offended he just burst out laughing.

When he laughed, really laughed...

Rose's skin prickled and she felt jumpy and weak at the same time, as if her bones were turning into hot liquid, no longer able to support her body.

'I'm glad you find that funny,' she said, and wondered if he, too, could detect the high-pitched panic in her voice. She wasn't quite sure why, but she badly needed to leave the room.

'Oh, I do...but you still haven't answered my question.'

'I didn't realise you'd asked one.' She gave a deep, exaggerated sigh, which she hoped would convey to him just how fed up she was with their conversation.

'About what you do after you finish discussing deep and meaningful things with your friends. In quiet rooms. Over some invigorating glasses of mineral water.' Nick grinned. In actual fact, he had headed to the office to have a break from the noise of the party, which was an event he had arranged solely for Lily's benefit. What an altruist he was turning out to be.

Work was always an absorbing diversion, but right now he couldn't care less about work because he was thoroughly enjoying himself. He was also more curious than ever to find out just a little bit more about the woman in front of him who was, right at this moment, barely managing to restrain herself from hitting him as hard as she could. He imagined that she could probably throw a pretty good punch. None of the usual female face-slapping before bursting into tears. More a sock to the jaw and then, when he was rubbing his face, another for good measure.

'I don't know what you're going on about and I think you should head back before they send out a search party.'

'Hardly likely considering most of them are far too inebri-ated to have even missed me, and what I'm going on about is whether, when your crazy late nights are over, you head back to your place for wild sex...do you?'

'I told you—that's none of your business.' Now she really needed to get out because something was happening and, while she didn't quite know what, she did know that it was...dangerous for her. And thankfully he stepped aside. He even opened the door for her, but before she could make a break to the safety of the crowded club he was leaning down to her; she could feel the warmth of his breath against her ear and it made her shiver.

'I take it that means *no*?'

She wanted to run but she didn't. She walked away, head held high, without bothering to dignify his smirking remark with an answer.

CHAPTER THREE

When Rose looked at the screen of her computer terminal she had the strangest sensation. Instead of seeing her programme run, she saw a face. *His* face. It was infuriating. Not only had the man got under her skin at the party nearly a week ago, but he was continuing to get under her skin when she should be concentrating on her work. She couldn't figure it out because she had pointedly avoided mentioning him to Lily and out of sight should have meant out of mind.

Just as well her office wasn't the sort of cosy little place where people might notice that she had been staring at the same code for the past fifteen minutes. In fact, the big pull about Fedco, when she had joined it five years previously, had been its size. Squatting like a giant patriarch on a retail site just outside London, it had been easily accessible by car, thereby enabling Rose to avoid the vagaries of the London transport system, and, once inside, she had been able to lose herself in the enormity of the building. Her friends all joked about leaving it behind, moving on to somewhere small, chic, designer and innovative where they could really exploit their talents, but in truth the thought of being at the cutting edge of technology in some small, upwardly mobile company terrified her. Small and cutting edge, in her head, spelt insecurity, whereas Fedco was as secure as they came, never mind that you were more a number than a face.

And where else could she sit scowling without someone telling her to get on with her work?

In between her scowls, she kept a sharp eye on the clock. She had never been one to clock-watch but she couldn't wait to leave the building and get back home, where she could put her feet up and drag her thoughts away from her sister's high-handed, arrogant boyfriend by watching a couple of hours of mindless television.

With fifteen minutes to go and just as she was finally beginning to get into her stride, an excited Maggie flew to her desk and announced, *sotto voce*, that there was a man waiting in Reception for her.

'What man?' Rose asked suspiciously, using the interruption as an excuse to switch off her computer and begin gathering her belongings.

'A dishy one.'

'I don't know any dish… Hang on, what exactly does he look like?' She could feel the colour crawling into her face.

'Oh, you know, tall and dark and drop dead gorgeous.'

'What the heck is *he* doing here?'

'*He* who?' Maggie looked as if swooning would become a real possibility within the next few minutes.

'*He* my sister's boyfriend.' Rose slammed some files into her briefcase and banged it shut. '*He* the most arrogant man on the face of the earth…*he* the person with the manners of a wild boar…*that he*…'

'Oh. Trust Lily to snap up another good one.' Maggie visibly wilted. 'Must be tough having a sister it's impossible to compete with…not that I meant…not that I mean…'

'I know what you meant, Mags, and you're right—on the looks front she's a hard act to follow…and she's nice with it…' Rose stood up, stuck on her coat and felt her stomach clench at the prospect of seeing Nick. 'Although I've got to say that this is the sort of man that no woman in her right mind would dream of competing for. One of those "love 'em and leave 'em" types of guys who see women as notches on their bedpost, the more the merrier.' The office was beginning to thin out as everybody began the exodus, off to enjoy the beginning of their weekend. 'I mean—' she leaned towards Maggie who gave a little yelp and stepped back '—the man is everything a woman should steer clear of—'

'Thanks for the endorsement.'

Nick's voice was so close to her that for a few seconds Rose didn't believe that she had actually heard him. He was standing right behind them. She turned around slowly and hoped that she was more composed than she felt. At any rate more composed than Maggie, who had launched into an awkward introduction followed by some stuttering apologies about having to dash, simultaneously backing away from Nick's unsmiling figure. Rose longed to do the same.

'What do you think you're doing here?' Attack, she decided, was the best form of defence. 'Is Lily with you?'

'No. Should she be?'

'Why are you here? Sneaking around?' He had obviously come straight from work and he looked amazing, unfairly sexy considering he had probably spent his day at a desk somewhere. Wherever it was that very rich people spent their days. At the end of a tiring working day, she always seemed to look like something the cat dragged in. Rumpled hair that had spent the day progressively rebelling against clips and elastic bands, lip gloss that had disappeared some time between her morning snack and lunch-time baguette, face that was shiny under the fluorescent lighting.

'We need to…have a chat about your sister…'

'Why?' Panic slammed into her. From experience, whenever someone had said to her that they needed to have a little chat, the little chat had never heralded good news. When she was growing up, Tony and Flora had always preceded their next, big, new adventure with a little chat. 'What's wrong?'

'Shall we take this conversation somewhere else?' He would return to those insults of hers later. For the moment, he would see to it that they leave the bustling confines of her office. He didn't have to glance around to know that he was attracting some very curious stares and, while this didn't bother him in the slightest, he suspected it would give her ample ammunition to attack him for disrupting her life.

He wondered what he was doing here. In fact, he wondered how his highly ordered existence had become so embroiled, in such a short space of time, with two sisters whom he had not known from Adam a month ago. The one, yes, he could understand. Lily was beautiful, sweet-natured and helping her had been a balm for him after the annoyance of his last relationship.

But her sister?

'No. I don't want to go with you anywhere. Whatever you have to say can be said right here.' Drugs? Debt? Pregnancy? Lord, what if Lily was pregnant with his child and too embarrassed to break the news herself? Rose tried to remember just how long Nick had been on the scene.

'Come on.'

'I'm not going anywhere with you.'

'Right. In that case, I'll just stroll out and leave you to stew in your own stubborn stupidity, shall I? You would rather make a point than listen to anything I have to say.'

'That's not true. It's just that I…can't leave yet. I still have heaps of work to do.'

'Wearing your coat? With your computer switched off?'

Rose flushed and looked away. The more she argued with the man, the more she sensed a lively interest from the dwindling number of her colleagues still around. 'Why didn't Lily come herself? Is she in trouble?'

'She…just seemed reluctant to tell you…this herself so I volunteered to do it on her behalf… Now, let's get out of here.'

It only took them five minutes to make it out of the building, but it could have been five hours. Why would Lily be reluctant to talk to her? They had always talked about everything. At least until this man had come along.

She shot him a look of pure resentment.

'You'll have to put up with my driving, I'm afraid.'

'My driver's waiting. We'll use him. I can deliver you back to your car later.'

Rose opened her mouth to protest and realised that he was waiting for the predictable objection.

'Okay.'

'*Okay?* Does that mean that you're not going to launch into a feminist rant about being able to drive yourself?'

'I never launch into feminist rants,' Rose said hotly. 'I just stand up for the things I believe in.'

'You shoot your mouth off.'

'I do not shoot my mouth off and I resent being told that I do.'

'And I don't much like the fact that you're gossiping about me behind my back. I'm obviously on your mind if you feel so strongly about me.'

'You are *not* on my mind!' They had reached his car, how she had no idea because she had been so wrapped up in defending herself.

Nick pulled open the passenger door for her and she slid primly inside, making sure, he noted, to wrap her coat very tightly around her, as if depending on it for protection.

It was out of keeping for him to ever leave work at the ridiculous hour of four forty-five, but he wasn't regretting his decision. Apart from the fact that he was doing Lily a favour, he was also enjoying himself with her sister. His palate, after years of getting precisely what and whom he wanted, was jaded. Rose, with her bristling, yapping aggression, was a novelty and who was he to resist the allure of the new?

He had also been curious to see the people she worked with, not that that had been possible given the size of the place.

'Where can we go?'

'At five-thirty?'

'Maybe we should just head back to your house. It's close enough.'

'No!' Overreacting again. And also forgetting about the little chat because she had been so wrapped up bickering. All fodder for his oversized ego. 'There's a brasserie about half an hour away. Joe's Brasserie. On Fields Road. I guess there's as good a place as any.' She turned away and stared out of the window, acutely conscious of his muscular thigh way too close to hers for comfort. Just being alone with the man in this confined space made her feel guilty. He belonged to Lily and to Lily's world. She shouldn't even recognise his physical attributes, although she gratefully accepted that she was human, after all, and, anyway, she disliked him intensely so what did it matter?

'You're tense. Why? Does it make you nervous sitting in this car with me?'

'Why should it?' Rose turned to look at him and blinked away the disconcerting impact his shadowed, angled face had on her. 'I'm tense because I don't know what you're going to tell me but I have a feeling that I won't like it.'

'In that case, take your mind off the possibilities and tell me about your job. I didn't expect you to work for such a large organisation.'

Rose shrugged. She didn't want to talk about herself or her job, but she couldn't see a way around it. 'I like it there. The size doesn't bother me. Anyway, don't tell me that your offices are sweet and small and cosy.'

Nick laughed under his breath. 'Better designed.'

'How?' Rose asked grudgingly, interested to find out how a big clump of concrete and glass could be designed into something less soulless than Fedco.

'Clever use of partitions and copious amounts of plants.'

'Right. And you did that yourself?'

'I approved it at every stage, yes. Does that jar with your picture of me striding through offices, whipping the employees and making sure that they're chained to their desks until I tell them that it's time to leave?'

'Yes, as a matter of fact it does.'

Nick laughed louder and gave her a brief, appreciative glance. When he sifted through his extensive repertoire of women, he couldn't think of a single one who had ever made him laugh.

'In that case, accept my apologies. Is this the place you were talking about?'

Rose nodded, pleased to see that it was already beginning to get busy. Brasseries in London never seemed to be quiet, and that suited her because she didn't want that weird, discomforting feeling she got when she was alone with him.

And that laugh had done something in her, made her feel oddly hot and uncomfortable.

'So,' she said without preamble as soon as they were seated at the circular chrome table and a waitress had taken their order. Orange juice for her and a lager for him. 'What is it that you wanted to tell me about Lily?'

'You're very good at cutting to the chase,' Nick commented drily. 'How much has she told you about…our relationship?'

'We don't discuss you.'

'Strange, considering you seem to discuss me freely with everyone else.'

Rose went pink but held his gaze. 'I don't think she would appreciate some of the things I might have to say and I can't put her in a position where she feels that she's having to take sides.'

'How big-minded of you.' Did the woman have no social graces? he wondered.

'I know you've been meeting up,' Rose ploughed on, 'but I don't know how serious it is. Are you telling me that it's…serious?'

'Oh, very serious indeed.' Nick sat back and took one long sip of lager, enjoying its coldness. 'I think it's now your cue to warn me off because I'm such a big, bad wolf.'

'Lily could have told me this herself.'

'Maybe she's scared of making a stand for herself because you've never allowed her to.'

'Is that what she told you?'

'I'm reading between the lines.'

'Then don't bother. You don't know anything about us.'

'I don't need case notes to see what's in front of my nose. You've always made the rules and Lily has always obeyed them.'

'If she's pregnant, then I expect you to do the honourable thing and marry her.'

For the first time in his life, Nick found himself lost for something to say and Rose watched his stunned expression without saying a word, waiting for him to be the first to break the silence. He had an annoying habit of throwing her into a tizzy and making her gabble like someone who couldn't operate the brake pedals on their mouth, but she could tell from his face that she had thrown him into a hole and she wasn't about to help fish him out.

This was the thing she feared the most—that Lily would do something stupid like fall for the man, hook, line and sinker. She hadn't seen her sister actually being even more stupid and getting herself pregnant, but if she had then Rose would be there, as she always had been, to lend the helping, guiding hand.

'You think that...' Nick shook his head incredulously. 'Shooting your mouth off again. Do you ever think before you speak?'

'What am I supposed to think?' Rose demanded, unfazed by his attack. 'You accost me at work—'

'I was doing you a favour.'

'You accost me at work, where, incidentally, you have no right to be, and insinuate that there's something you have to tell me that's so awful that my own sister just can't tell me herself.'

'And you think that pregnancy is the most awful thing that could happen to a woman.'

'No, of course I don't. When two people love each other and have a stable relationship, then pregnancy is the most beautiful thing that could happen, but in Lily's case...' She glared at him because he had started staring at her as though she had begun speaking in tongues.

'You surprise me. I never thought you would have subscribed to the Happy Ever After fairy tale.'

'What *I* subscribe to or don't subscribe to is beyond the point,' Rose snapped. 'The fact is this—if Lily is pregnant—'

'Oh, for God's sake. She's not pregnant.' Nick leaned towards her, resting both his elbows on the table, and Rose fought not to pull back because the sheer force of his personality was so overwhelming. 'Let's get one thing straight here, Rose. I'm not a complete fool. I'm no shrinking violet when it comes to the opposite sex, but I make sure to always, but always, use protection. Believe me, the very last thing I would ever want would be to find myself cornered into marriage by a scheming woman who gets herself pregnant so that she can manoeuvre her way into my bank account.'

'That is the most cynical thing I've ever heard in my life!'

Nick looked at Rose furiously. Respect was something he had commanded from other people for all of his adult life. Respect and admiration were the two things he had commanded from women. This one, white faced and disapproving, not only lacked both, but was actually sitting in judgement on him. Him! Nick Papaeliou, a man whose ability to instil fear was legendary.

He was finding it difficult to believe his ears.

'You can't be a very happy, well-adjusted human being if you think that the only reason a woman would want to go out with you would be because of your bank balance.'

'No. I am not sitting here listening to this.'

'And to imagine that a woman would be conniving enough to get herself pregnant just because she wanted your money…'

At long last his formidable self-control began once again gathering pace, solidifying into icy steel. 'Do you live in the real world at all, Rose? Or are you the archetypal computer nerd everyone reads about? The one who can do amazing things with software but hasn't got a clue when it comes to real

ife? Because you must be wildly naïve to think that money
isn't the thing that makes the world go round. I have met more
gold-diggers in my life than you have had hot dinners.'

'In which case I feel very sorry for you.'

'I think I need another drink.' He summoned across a
waitress, keeping his eyes fixed on Rose. 'Lily isn't pregnant.
That's all you need to know.'

'That's a relief,' Rose said sincerely, thinking it prudent not
to tack on that his take on women in general left a whole lot
to be desired. Yes, as she calmed down, she could see that he
had a point, that women might find his wealth a pretty
powerful aphrodisiac. Although, a little voice inside her acknowledged, he must know that with his looks he could be as
poor as a church mouse and still have the female population
lusting after him. 'And I apologise if I…went off on a bit of
a tangent just then…'

'A bit of a tangent?'

'You were saying some pretty emotive things.'

Nick wondered how he had suddenly been cast as the
villain of the piece when all he had done was to be perfectly
truthful with her. He should have remembered that he wasn't
dealing with a normal, twenty-first-century woman.

'Apology accepted,' he grated.

'So why don't you tell me why…what you wanted to
discuss with me…?'

'I'm very fond of your sister,' Nick began, 'but before you
jump in both feet first, let me just add that she and I are not
having a relationship. At least, not in the sense in which you
probably expect that we are.'

'What do you mean?'

'Do I have to spell it out for you?' He impatiently tugged
off his tie and undid the top two buttons of his shirt. Was it

his imagination or was this place sweltering? 'Lily and I are
not having sex. We have never had sex. It has not been that
kind of a relationship between us…' Since that made a first
for him, he was inordinately proud of the fact that he was
managing to sustain a great, platonic relationship with a beautiful woman. Not only that, but he felt no stirrings of attraction whatsoever. It had occurred to him that his relationships
had become more problematic as the years had progressed.
Women had invariably wanted more than he could offer and
was it really worth the hassle?

'What kind of relationship is it, then?' Rose asked.

'She's a sweet kid. I know a lot of people in the industry
and I've been helping her.'

'Helping her do what?'

'Helping her with her career.'

'You mean putting her in touch with…' With whom?
Actors? Producers? Directors? Rose knew precious little
about what went on behind the scenes in the world of acting.
It was so far removed from the prosaic life she led.

'With people who could help her.'

'That's…very nice of you.' Frankly, she was slightly bewildered. 'Is that why you wanted to see me? Why couldn't Lily
have just told me all that herself? Instead of being so secretive about…everything?'

'Have you ever heard of Damien Hicks?'

'Should I have?'

'Just answer the question, Rose.'

'No.'

'Well, he's an up-and-coming film producer.'

A sense of humour inserted itself in between her bemusement as to where Nick was going with this conversation. 'Not many of those roaming around in my line of work. Do they have any distinguishing features I might identify them by?'

'They're fond of cigars,' Nick answered drily. He paused. 'I met Damien when one of my companies was doing an advertising shoot in the Maldives. Not really Damien's thing now, but five years ago he was just beginning to make his mark. He did the campaign for me and I helped him finance his first film. Just a short feature, but since then his rise has been meteoric. He likes working with new talent.'

'And Lily is new talent.' Rose smiled. 'She should have been jumping at the opportunity to tell me, after all the disappointments she's been through.'

'His new film needs a lead, Rose. Don't get me wrong, he's auditioned countless young hopefuls and has come to the conclusion that Lily is the one through no doing of mine. I introduced them, got him to give her a chance and she's done the rest.'

'Why do I get the feeling that there's a *but* lurking just around the corner?'

'But,' he said quietly, 'and this is why Lily was having a hard time discussing this with you...the part will be shot exclusively in America and there's more than a fifty-per-cent chance that, once she gets over there, she'll find herself caught up in the Hollywood industry. It's bigger, there are more opportunities and with a CV that starts with a Hicks movie...'

Rose knew that the colour was draining away from her face.

'I know this is probably unexpected and not particularly pleasant...'

'And Lily wants to go to America to live?'

'She wants to give it a go, see what happens.'

'Right.'

'She also wants to go with your blessing.'

'Right.' Rose barely had any memories of a life without her

sister. They had always been there for one another and she had never given much thought to the day when they would go their different ways. That had been a bridge waiting to be crossed and she had never considered how she would cross it when it did finally loom on the horizon. 'Of course she has my blessing. I…I only want what's best for her and if there's a chance that she could make her dreams come true out there, well…who am I to stand in her way?' The words were right but the hollowness inside made her feel sick.

'Come on. Let's get out of here.'

'Yes.' She stood up and took a deep breath. 'But there's no need for you to come. You've done what you came to do and you can leave me now. I'm capable of taking care of myself.'

'Try looking in the mirror and then telling yourself that.'

Rose turned away and fumbled for her bag. She couldn't help but think that this was all his fault even though she knew that the chance he had given Lily was the greatest favour he could have granted. Was she so selfish that she would rather have Lily stay at home than take flight and find her dreams somewhere else?

But when she thought of her sister living across the Atlantic, she wanted to burst into tears.

She made a few feeble protests about wanting him to go, but she didn't put up much of a fight when she found herself back in his car being driven to her house.

'Go and sit. I'll get you something to drink.'

'I'm not thirsty.' Rose finally surfaced from her thoughts and tried to shoot him her widest smile. 'And look…' She pointed at her smile. 'Doesn't this prove that I'm just fine?'

'Lily will be back shortly. Do you want her to see you freaked out like this?'

'I am not freaked out.' She glared at him through the smile.

It was so hard to do both and in the middle of trying she felt her lower lip wobble and she knew what was coming. Not even closing her eyes could squeeze back the tears, and then she felt his arms go around her and, worse, felt herself comforted by his strength as he enveloped her.

Nick felt her melt against him and drew her as tightly to him as he could. He had never had the benefit of siblings and, yes, he had known, just as Lily had known, that Rose would be upset, but up close he was staggered by the power of her affection for her sister. He could actually feel her tears soaking into his shirt and she was sobbing, but quietly, as if ashamed at making so much noise.

He felt in his trouser pocket and located a clean handkerchief, which he pressed against her cheek, and that seemed to staunch some of her tears although when she drew back he very nearly wanted to pull her against him again.

His only experiences with weeping women had been at the end of a relationship and their tears had irritated him. What did one say to a woman at a time like this?

'I'll make sure you get the hankie back.' Rose spared him the dilemma of finding the right words. She gave him a watery smile and he did the only thing he could think of doing. He wiped a stray tear from her face with his finger, which made her remember who he was and she stepped back a little further.

'Thank you for the lift back.' Rose gathered herself sufficiently to look him in the eye. She could see the sympathy there and felt a complete and utter fool because she knew what he must be thinking: that the loser of a sister was so thrown by the thought of being on her own that she had broken down and blubbed like a baby. 'I'm glad that I've got that out of my system and, honestly, I really am happy for Lily and hope that she gets everything she deserves.'

'I'm going to pour you something strong. Or would you prefer tea?' He couldn't remember the last time he had made a cup of tea.

'I would prefer you to leave, actually.'

'No.'

'No?' Some of her old fire returned and Nick felt quietly satisfied, although he still knew that he was going to stay with her. At least until she was back to her full vitriolic self, trying to shoot him down in flames. He was fast discovering a masochistic streak in him he had never known existed.

'Go sit…' He waved in the direction of the lounge. 'I'll be five minutes.'

Less, in actual fact, as he decided to dispense with the tea-making and pour her a stiff drink instead. Much better for the nerves, he told himself.

'It was just the shock of what you said,' Rose greeted him defensively, half standing as he handed her the drink. 'What's this?'

'An old family remedy for stressed nerves.'

She sniffed the glass. 'Called?'

'Vodka and a touch of whatever juice I happened to find in the fridge.' He sat on the sofa by her and watched as she took a tentative mouthful. 'Lily is actually contemplating turning down Damien's offer if you find it too upsetting having her leave,' Nick said quietly.

'That would be mad.' Rose looked at him and sipped a little more. 'I can't believe that you've been on the scene less than a month and our lives are being turned upside down.'

'I wondered when you would get around to blaming me,' Nick said coolly.

Rose, remembering how she had felt holding onto him and sobbing, cast him a baleful look. 'I wasn't blaming you. I was just making a passing remark.' She had felt weak and helpless and protected and vulnerable, all things she had thought she had left behind when their parents had died and Tony and Flora had taken them in. For that alone, she felt resentful.

'Ever thought that sometimes life is richer when you step out of your comfort zone?'

'No,' Rose said bluntly. 'There was quite a bit of stepping out of comfort zones when I was young and I don't remember any of it making my life feel any richer.'

'Your aunt and uncle…'

'Wandering the highways and byways. You try facing changes every six months and then tell me how great it is stepping out of comfort zones.'

'But Lily may have something of the adventurer in her…'

Rose heard the affection in his voice and, yes, she could see why he felt protective towards her sister. Most people did. She had gentle, girlish, winning ways. For the first time in her life she felt a stab of pure, uncharitable jealousy, which made her draw her breath in sharply.

'Yes, you're right, she does,' Rose said coolly. 'And I don't.' Which made her a bore in his eyes because the women who peopled his life, the women he was drawn to, weren't boring worker bees like her, they were the bright, sparkly, adventurous fireflies that flitted from light to light. 'Now—' she stood up '—I really would rather you weren't here when Lily gets home. I want to have a talk with her in private and you needn't worry that I'm going to do anything that might make her change her mind. I'm happy for her.'

Nick reluctantly rose to his feet. He had glimpsed through a little window of vulnerability and, strangely for him, because vulnerability wasn't a character trait he found attractive in a woman, he wanted to see a bit more, but Rose was already walking towards the door, just the pinkness round her eyes to account for her crying jag.

'I don't expect I'll be seeing much of you again,' she told him politely as he slipped on his coat and felt in the pockets, out of habit, for the keys to his apartment.

'Why do you say that?'

'Because I imagine Lily will leave sooner rather than later. You didn't specify a time, but I guess cutting edge movie producers don't sit around tapping their feet waiting for their plots to go cold.'

'No, I guess they don't.'

'So I may not get a chance to tell you that I'd rather you don't breathe a word to Lily about my…my…'

'Crying? Breaking down?'

'My little loss of self-control.' Rose stuck her chin up and met his eyes without blinking.

She was positively shuffling him towards the front door and she pulled it wide open before he could do the sensible thing and lean against it. Because suddenly and inexplicably, he didn't want to go. Not just yet. But there was no choice.

'I won't tell her. You have my word.'

Rose nodded and, without saying a word, she quietly closed the door in his face.

CHAPTER FOUR

COMPOSING emails to Lily was becoming a combination of subtlety and creative fiction.

After Lily had been abroad for three weeks, it had become clear to Rose that life in the fast lane was suiting her sister. She waxed lyrical about the movie she was making, devoted pages to telling her all about the fabulously talented Damien Hicks and the groovy, exciting people she was working with. The flat she was sharing with four other girls, all newcomers like herself, was cheap but apparently called a condo and had a swimming pool. The adjective amazing had become a staple word in her vocabulary. Everything was amazing from the movie to the people to life in general, and Rose was relieved and pleased that it was all working out for her sister.

Which, unfortunately, didn't solve the financial problems that seemed to have been saving themselves for the minute Lily waved her fond goodbye to British soil.

The bathroom had sprung a leak, which, as the plumber had ominously told Rose, revealed all the makings of a dated system that could be patched up but would really need to be replaced at some point. Rose had opted for the patching-up job. Then the washing machine had collapsed, which had meant a new one. And now, sitting in the kitchen, she could see a damp patch on the ceiling, which didn't augur well for the dated plumbing system or, for that matter, her rapidly depleting savings account.

Rose groaned. She wondered how she could phrase the words 'need money' so that her sister didn't go into spasms of guilt and worry. Lily had already apologised for not being able to send any over, but she would just as soon as she could. At the moment, she was being paid enough to cover her rent and build a lifestyle that befitted an up-and-coming Hollywood actress, which left precious little for the crumbling house she had left behind.

Rose didn't begrudge her a minute of the enjoyment she was having. Lily deserved it. But her single income was being tested to its limits and it was getting harder to keep writing her all 'fine here' emails when the roof was falling down.

Literally.

One week later, with the damp patch still making small inroads even though the bath was out of commission, she sat at her kitchen table to the sounds of plumbers banging upstairs and the horrible prospect of going to check on them so that she could find her floorboards up and her cool magnolia walls covered with dust. They had been at it for the past two days, putting in a new, updated system. She had not dared enquire as to the cost but the sight of the shiny new copper pipes had made her blood run cold.

Lily was, according to her email yesterday, heading off for two weeks to Arizona where some of the movie was being filmed. Rose knew that she had tried to de-glamorise the whole thing, but it wasn't hard to read between the lines that she was bubbling over with excitement.

While I sit here, she thought glumly, like Chicken Little waiting for the sky to fall down. Everything else seemed to be.

The sound of the doorbell managed, just, to penetrate the sounds of the banging and Rose vaguely wondered what life had in store for her next. A kindly neighbour coming to tell her that her car had been vandalised? Maybe they had noticed a spot of terminal subsidence on an outside wall?

She pulled open the door, dressed in her very best dungarees, bedroom slippers and old jumper because dust and fine clothing just didn't go hand in hand, and there he was. The man she had avoided mentioning in all the emails she had sent her sister, the man who kept popping into her head at all the wrong times, even though she had robustly told herself that she was well rid of him.

Her response to him, lounging indolently against the door frame, finger poised as if about to summon her again, was immediate and powerful. Her stomach constricted and her eyes widened, swiftly and unconsciously taking in his lean, muscular frame and those killer sea-green eyes that seemed to burn holes through her. She had to make a mental effort to gather herself together.

'Hullo.' Pause. 'What are you doing here?'

'Still getting to the point, I see. What's going on?'

'What do you mean?' She followed his curious glance behind her and shrugged. 'Oh. The noise. Just a bit…of repair work.'

'Are you going to invite me in?'

'Has Lily told you to get in touch with me?' She had been careful not to mention a word about her financial problems, but who knew? Maybe her sister had picked up on something and, innocent that she was, might have mentioned to Nick, Nick with the heart of gold who had done so much for her, that perhaps he could just pop his head round the door and make sure that Rose was okay.

Rose instantly felt like a charity case and gripped the door knob a little harder.

'I was in the area.'

'Really? I wouldn't have thought that this would be the sort of area you would just happen to be passing through.'

'Stop arguing, Rose, and open the door.' Getting fed up with her non-argument, he pushed the door and strode in, not leaving her the option of slamming it in his face.

Nick, for the first time in years practising celibacy, was aware of the shameful truth, which was that he had been thinking on and off about her for the past few weeks. His life had been as busy and hectic as ever, his work taking him abroad, as it always did, on a regular basis, but every so often he had caught himself conjuring up her face and wondering what she was up to.

Gentle prodding had eventually elicited from Lily something he could respond to. Rose, Lily had told him in all confidence, had not sounded herself when they had last spoken on the phone. She had said all the right things, that everything was fine, but she had sounded anxious.

Nick had reacted like a man who suddenly discovered the site of an itch and realised that he could reach to scratch it. Sitting on his leather swivel chair, feet carelessly propped up on his gleaming, mahogany desk, he had immediately and piously promised to look in on her.

'You wouldn't want to have filming ruined because you're worried about what's going on over here,' he had soothed. His prospect of a weekend of solid work, interrupted only by a stuffy Saturday night do, which he had reluctantly agreed to purely for diplomatic reasons, suddenly brightened considerably.

He wasn't entirely sure why he could be bothered to hunt down a woman who rubbed him up the wrong way, but when it came to members of the opposite sex he rarely questioned his responses, safe in the knowledge that his gut feelings had rarely, if ever, let him down. Granted his gut feelings were usually wrapped up in the normal, testosterone-driven desires for a sexual relationship, but the fact that Rose was out of the ordinary in that respect didn't put him off. She had been on his mind, for whatever reason, and the fastest way to solve that problem would be to hunt her down. And Lily was a very handy go-between, giving him an excuse he might not otherwise have had.

'What the hell is that banging all about?'

'I told you. Repair work. Minor.' Rose bristled at the sight of those fabulous eyes sweeping along the banister, up to where a fine shimmer of dust obscured the small upstairs corridor. She wondered what her sister had said to him. God, what if she had begged Nick to check up on her? Lily would have thought nothing of asking such a favour because, in her eyes, Nick wasn't a shark but some innocuous little minnow, someone who would be happy to do her a small favour. In Lily's world, everyone was potentially sweet and good because she herself was.

Rose determined that as soon as her sister returned to England, she would personally teach her the ways of the world. Lily might have oodles more experience when it came to men, but her insight into human nature was sadly lacking.

'Doesn't sound minor.'

'You still haven't told me what you're doing here. If Lily put you up to this, then there's no need to be concerned.'

'Even though your house is falling down?'

'My house is not falling down!'

Nick had forgotten how easily the woman bristled. He had also forgotten how amusing he found the trait. It made a refreshing change from his normal interaction with women, which went along all the usual courses that inevitably led to bed. Bed and all its attendant complications, which he was determined to avoid, at least for a while.

'Why don't you get me a cup of coffee and tell me all about it? You look stressed.'

Rose gaped. Of course she was stressed. An army of plumbers was currently bankrupting her and now, on top of that, the last man on earth she wanted to see had waltzed through her front door, brimming over with tea and sympathy because her dear, well-intentioned and hopelessly misguided sister had asked him to. Who wouldn't be stressed?

And on top of that, she was now embarrassingly aware of her clothes, which advertised someone who was in serious danger of imminent arrest by the fashion police.

While he, she noticed sourly, fashionably dressing down in faded jeans and a rugby sweater, still managed to look fantastic.

'I'm more stressed now that you've shown up,' Rose told him and Nick immediately jumped on the slip-up.

'So you're admitting you're stressed out. Lily did say you didn't sound your normal self when she spoke to you on the phone.'

Rose mentally strangled her sister. 'Hence you were coerced into rushing over here just to make sure I wasn't about to jump off the nearest bridge.'

'That's taking it too far.' There was an almighty thump from the direction of the dust and Rose groaned, waiting for Andy's voice to summon her up, probably to confront yet another unexpected problem. Like a routine trip to the dentist, which turned out to reveal a nightmare of hidden problems, her house was beginning to revel in showing its age. A little crack there, a small spot of damp here and suddenly it was as if it had given up the fight and was now determined to fall down around her ears. And as she mounted the stairs she could already see from the grim look on Andy's face that more bad news was on the way.

'Sorry, Rose.'

Behind her she was aware that Nick had followed in her hurried wake and she could sense his attention moving up a gear.

'We've discovered something a little unfortunate…'

Rose was too afraid to ask, so she stared at him in mute silence while he shook his head and gave her a look of such profound sympathy that she feared the worst.

'Asbestos.'

Rose saw the very last of her savings flutter through the window and she balled her hand into a fist and clenched it under her chin. 'How can that be?'

'Lodged under the floorboards,' Andy said kindly. 'Nothing to look at, but I can spot it a mile away. It's not everywhere but for the moment we're going to have to put everything back in place until it's sorted. We're not trained to remove it.'

'I don't suppose you're going to tell me that you're joking.'

'Wish I could, love.'

'And I guess you don't know how much it'll cost to have it removed?'

He shrugged while behind him his guys were efficiently putting the floorboards back down. 'Best not lose sleep over that one, considering you've got no option…'

Rose saw them out and was too despondent to care whether Nick was hovering in the background with his uninvited sympathy. She didn't even care that he had been dispatched to check on her as if she were incapable of looking after herself without Lily around.

'So—' she turned to face him, slamming the front door shut

on her plumbing messengers of bad tidings '—there you go. House collapsing. Money disappearing. Stress levels high. In other words lots to report back to Lily, although I'm hoping you'll dredge up sufficient compassion to know that I would rather she enjoyed all the opportunities opening up for her in America without having to worry about what's happening to me back here.'

'How long has this place been falling down?'

Rose shrugged. 'Weeks. It's been saving itself for Lily's departure.' She sighed, too tired and depressed to argue at his presence in the house, allowing him to witness her plight. She found that he was leading the way to the kitchen, manoeuvring around the cupboards until there was a mug of sweet tea in front of her, and she gratefully swallowed a mouthful.

'And you never breathed a word to her because you didn't want her to worry.'

'There was no point. She would have rushed back over here and that would have been the end of her career, everything she has worked so hard for.'

'So you decided to shoulder the stress on your own.' He had shoved back his stool so that he could stretch out his long legs and was looking at her thoughtfully. 'Except now you're left facing bills you can't afford.'

'I'll just have to put in a bit more overtime,' Rose snapped, railing against any suggestion of pity.

'Quite a bit more,' Nick commented drily, raising his eyes to the ceiling and the source of her misfortune. Frankly he had zero firsthand experience of a woman who had to work literally to keep the roof over her head.

'Yes, well, it's not impossible.' She stared at him sourly and with inspired accuracy continued, in a tight voice, 'I guess this is a completely different world to the one you're used to, where problems get fixed with the snap of your fingers. I don't suppose you know too many women who face a struggle to pay unexpected bills and can't afford the little luxuries you would take for granted.'

'Attacking me isn't going to solve your financial crisis.'

Rose didn't care for the word crisis. It was a little too evocative for comfort. 'You have to go. I need to phone my bank manager.'

'On a Saturday?'

'I don't know why I didn't think of that before. Of course, I can call my bank manager and take out a loan.'

'Which will have to be repaid.'

'But at least I'll be able to afford the repair work,' Rose pointed out wearily. 'And if you're going to sit there and state the obvious then you can finish that cup of tea and go.'

'And in the meantime, where do you intend to live?'

'Here, of course.'

'Dust everywhere? Hidden dangers under the floorboards? And what about when you get the men in to clear the asbestos? What then? Hang around in a mask?'

Rose felt tears of frustration and anger prick the backs of her eyes. 'Oh, just leave me alone.'

'So you can wallow in self-pity?'

'I do not wallow in self-pity,' she flung back at him through gritted teeth, shaken out of her despondency by the force of rage. 'I've got my solution and as soon as the banks open on Monday, I'll be there.'

'You can't live here.'

'Oh, you're right,' she sniped with dripping sarcasm. 'I'll just get my butler to book me in at the Savoy until everything's sorted out.'

Nick stifled a grin. 'Better idea. You need money and I have it.'

'Forget it, Nick. You might do favours for my sister, but I don't need anything from you.' She gave him a mutinous look, which he chose to ignore.

Was there any woman as stubborn as this one? He felt a sudden desire to be the one who controlled the reins and melted the fortresses she had erected everywhere around herself.

'You're letting your emotions talk and emotions never solved anything. If you run to the bank for a loan, you'll spend the next few years paying it back along with the crippling interest accrued.'

'So instead I take the money from you? And in return you get what?'

A vivid image of her lying naked in his bed presented itself and he blinked it away.

'You can't hide a problem of this magnitude from your sister. You might want to protect her from everything harsh that life can throw at her, but she deserves to know the truth about what's happening over here. Give her enough credit not to be a complete fool and come hurtling back to England when she knows that it wouldn't solve anything. If she finds out that you've been keeping this from her, she'll feel betrayed.'

'Don't pretend you know my sister better than I do,' Rose retorted, but his words set up a chain of thoughts that began to gnaw away at her composure. She had always been the one looking out for Lily, but where did concern end and smothering begin?

Uncertainty shadowed her face and Nick, spotting it, jumped in. 'I'm not pretending anything, but you have to tell her. Course she'd want to fly over, make sure you were okay, but she might not if…'

'If what?'

'If she knew that I was looking out for you.' Since when had he ever looked out for any woman? The rules of his game had always been simple. No dependency, no strings attached. Rose ignited some other feeling in him. She didn't conform to his ideas of physical feminine beauty so, whatever weird stirrings he had occasionally felt in her presence, he was certain it wasn't lust. But whatever it was, it was certainly novel and to his jaded palate the thought of something new was strangely alluring.

'Oh, please.'

'I am trying to help you out here,' Nick told her irritably. 'Why can't you just accept it?'

'I don't see you as the kind of guy who helps damsels in distress,' Rose pointed out, omitting to mention the fine print, which was unless they looked like Lily or unless he wanted something from them. 'You think you ought to offer assistance because you feel guilty. By some weird coincidence, you happen to show up when all this…' she gestured vaguely around her '…is going on and you think you ought to do something because you have a relationship with Lily. You feel sorry for the plain, ungainly sister left behind trying to cope.'

'I'm not suggesting I hand over the money and walk away. You seem to forget I'm a businessman.'

'Well, what are you offering, then? Not that there's any chance I'm going to take you up on your offer.'

'Because you're a stubborn fool.'

'Because I don't like the thought of being indebted to anyone.'

'Except the bank.'

'That's different.' Rose flushed, feeling boxed in by his clever use of words.

Novelty value was fast turning into challenge and it was invigorating. 'Take a couple of months off work…'

'Take a couple of months off work?' Was the man a complete lunatic? 'Have you been listening to a word I've been saying?' She shook her head in disgust and snatched up the mugs, carrying them off to the sink. Nick swivelled round so that he was looking at her and, while he was staring, she spun around and leant against the kitchen sink, arms folded. 'You know what's happening here, the financial strain I'm suddenly under, and your breezy solution is for me to have time off work? That activity that pays the bills?'

'How much do they pay you a month?'

Rose went pink. Wasn't discussing of salary the final taboo? Not that this man would skirt round a taboo if his life depended on it.

'Well? No need to be shy.'

'What I earn is none of your concern.' She should have asked for a pay rise months ago. She was damned good at her job and worked a lot longer hours than all of her colleagues. If only she had had a crystal ball foretelling her huge household bills were on the horizon she might have been more assertive during her appraisal. She reluctantly told him, knowing that he would just carry on sitting there until she did. He didn't laugh, as she had expected him to. Instead he looked at her for a few seconds, as though weighing up something in his head.

'I'm branching out,' he told her, 'going into the leisure business. Corporate investment and the money markets pay the bills but I've conquered that challenge. Now, I'm investing some of my own reserves in building up a boutique hotel portfolio.'

Rose thought of the reserves she was investing in—making sure she didn't wake up with the ceiling on her pillow.

'What's a boutique hotel?'

'Something very small and exquisite and strictly for people

who don't want to be surrounded by hundreds of people every time they step out of their bedroom.'

'Don't tell me…strictly for the very rich because privacy costs.'

'Of course. Like I said, I'm a businessman. I'm starting with one in Borneo.'

'Borneo,' she echoed sceptically.

'Trust me…the next must-go-to destination. It'll be small, eco friendly and built to the highest standards. And here's where you come in…' Nick paused. 'You spend the next two months running the show. You set up the computer system for all the accounting et cetera, you liaise with the architects—'

'I don't know the first thing about…hotels. I can't even think when the last time I stayed in one was.'

'Which I'll make sure to put right,' Nick murmured. 'Think about it, Rose. You won't be able to live here while work's being done… I'm offering to relieve you of the stress of living out of an overnight bag on a friend's floor. I'll put you up in three separate hotels in London over the next two months so that you can have firsthand experience of what makes a good one work, and in addition I'll pay you double what you would have been earning. In return, you can try your hand at something other than sitting in front of a terminal all day long.'

Nick, who donated vast sums to charity on an annual basis, had only ever had nodding acquaintance with altruism on a personal level and he was finding that it felt good to be at the giving end of largesse. In truth, he could increase her salary multiple times and not notice the difference to his bank balance, but he was shrewd enough to know that there was a thin line between a reasonable proposition and a contemptuous act of charity for which he would probably find his hand roundly bitten off.

Because this woman snapped and snarled and yapped and bit and he was looking forward to taming her. He decided to look on it as his pet project. All work and no play…well, he knew the saying well enough and, as he wasn't playing at the moment, he would devote all of his formidable attention to digging underneath that prickly exterior to the woman inside. And doing her a good turn in the bargain by fishing her out of a pretty nasty hole.

'Don't you have people who could do the job for you?'

'Don't you have any ability to just say thank you and go away to count your blessings?'

'Why do I get the feeling that there's an ulterior motive to your offer?' Rose asked. She felt driven to find holes in his proposal even though the rational side of her was already calculating the benefits of what he was offering. She had worked long enough for the company to know that they would not have a problem in giving her unpaid leave while she sorted out her domestic situation and the thought of something different was appealing. Stepping out of her comfort zone was appealing. Appealing and frightening at the same time.

'Because you're inherently suspicious.' Nick shrugged and stood up. 'If you're not interested, then I'll leave you to get on with the messy business of sorting your house out with the help of your friendly bank manager.'

'Wait!'

She raced behind him as he headed for the front door, glancing sideways as she did so, where the shimmer of dust in the air reminded her of the generosity of his offer.

'What if I fail? I have no experience…'

'Have faith in yourself. You won't fail. I take it that that's a yes?'

'I shall have to clear it with my boss.'

'And if you do take up this opportunity…' Nick lazily appraised her, from her worn bedroom slippers to the shapeless dungarees, which, he now thought, should only ever be worn by labourers on a building site '…you'll have to do something about your wardrobe.'

Rose went bright red. It occurred to her that actually working with the man might just prove to be more stressful than sorting out her situation without his help.

'I don't go to work in these clothes,' she said coolly. 'I put them on because anything else would have been stupid.' Lily would have managed to look fabulous in faded, old clothes but she had to stop comparing herself to Lily. 'If you don't think that I'm decorative enough to work with you, then you might as well tell me now because I don't intend to buy a brand-new wardrobe for a two-month stint. And also…' she drew herself up and stared him straight in the eyes '…if I do happen to work for you, then I don't want you to think that I'm doing it because I actually like you.'

'Very tactful.'

'I'm just being honest.'

'And, believe me, I find that very refreshing, especially in a woman.' He was so accustomed to women using their bodies and their wiles to get what they wanted that the metaphorical bucket of water Rose kept tipping over him was doing him no end of good. He even contemplated the possibility of taking a little time out to show her the ropes.

'There might be some travel involved,' he continued. 'Do you have a passport?'

Rose nodded as the parameters broadened around her.

'And because you'll be working for me directly, I will set you up with an office inside my place.'

'Whoa. Stop right there. I don't think that's a good idea at all.'

'Why not?'

'Because…because it would be a lot more professional for me to…ah…work in an office environment.' She envisaged somewhere imbued with his masculine scent, with the open door to his bedroom within throwing distance. She shied away from the image with an inward yelp of dismay.

'You'll be there on your own,' Nick said, amused at her discomfiture. 'And, face it, this is my private project. I can hardly bring you into the office, sit you down and not expect you to become an object of curiosity.'

'Well, you could explain…'

'Dangerous curiosity…' Nick expanded silkily, waiting in telling silence as her eyes widened. 'People would naturally assume that because I had brought you in to work on my personal project, we were an item.'

'An item?'

'Involved with one another. Going out. Lovers. Now, I don't much give a damn what other people think of me, but I don't bring my private life to work.'

'But you…we…we don't have a private life,' Rose protested, going bright red.

'Immaterial. Tongues will wag and I can't have my power diminished. Does that answer your objection?'

'Of course, I can see your point of view, but…you have to see mine as well…'

'And that is…?' He leaned against the door and stuck his hands into his pockets.

'Well…' Rose tried to think of a coherent argument that wouldn't make her sound prissy in the process. How could she explain that just standing next to him in her own house made her feel nervous and uncomfortable, so how much more difficult was it going to be when she was working in his?

'Your virtue is perfectly safe with me.' Nick grinned. 'Like I said, I won't be there during the day, and if you're scared of being around me in my apartment, then we can always catch up on neutral territory. There's a pub just around the corner. We can avoid the cubby-holes with the subdued lighting.'

'Of course I'm not scared of you.'

'Good, because there's no reason to be, nor is there any reason to feel uncomfortable in my presence.'

Mortified, Rose interpreted his slow, amused smile as his way of telling her that he wouldn't come near her if she happened to be the last woman on the face of the earth.

'I'll let you know after I've spoken to my boss. Tomorrow some time. Is that all right?' What was she letting herself in for?

One month into her new temporary job, she was fast finding out.

A chic five-star hotel tucked away in the bowels of Covent Garden was her first project for inspection. Her brief was to examine why it worked and in detail, with a weekly report to be compiled for Nick's scrutiny. That, in addition to checking out costs for everything under the sun that might possibly be needed in the construction of a hotel. There seemed to be a hundred people, all of whom she had to liaise with, and Nick, at the end of each day, expected perfect recall and written reports on everything.

He would sweep into his apartment at six-thirty and, although he had told her that she could clear off by five and email him with her findings, she had pretty quickly sussed that, whatever he said, he expected her to work until at least six-thirty and if necessary later.

And she didn't mind. She had thought, a lifetime ago it seemed, that she would be crammed into his small personal space and, like a cat on a hot tin roof, would spend every minute there in nervous expectation of his sudden entry. She had envisaged being surrounded by his private objects, which would intrude on her, a constant nagging and stomach-churning reminder of his overwhelming personality.

But his apartment, for starters, was vast. It was also peculiarly impersonal. The abstract paintings on the white walls gave no clue to the man except to indicate his wealth. There were no photos in frames or ornaments standing on shelves. Two cleaners came promptly at eight every morning, and departed at ten, leaving the apartment spotless. Her office was no makeshift affair. It was large and kitted out for serious work and, once there, Rose had no trouble concentrating.

And then, just as she was usually packing up to leave, he would sweep in. From the office, Rose would hear the slam of the front door and the jangle of keys as he carelessly tossed them on the granite kitchen counter. Then he would appear in the doorway, tugging at his tie, leaning against the doorframe and watching her for a few seconds in silence as she logged off the computer.

It was the time of day she had been dreading. Yet now, it was the time of day Rose waited for with a sense of heady, forbidden, crawling expectation.

Tonight was no exception and she felt her stomach churn with excitement as she heard him approach. She knew it was wrong but her attraction to him was something she just couldn't seem to stuff away somewhere conveniently out of reach. It had ambushed her from behind and her only defence against it was to hang onto her veneer of professional self-control.

'I've got those costings for you.' She had trained her eyes not to stare whenever he tugged his tie off, but, like recalcitrant kids, they still always managed to sneak a look at that glimpse of hard brown chest that was revealed as he undid the top two buttons of his shirt.

'And I've got something for you…' He walked towards her, waggling a piece of paper in his hand.

'What is it?'

'Have a look.' He gave her the envelope and leant on the computer terminal, watching as she slit it open. 'We're going on a trip.' He smiled slowly as she tipped her face up to stare at him. 'A little look-see at some prime land in Borneo.' He moved round so that he was behind her chair and then he bent towards her. Rose could feel his warm breath against her neck. 'Fish out the summer glad rags, Rose. It's going to be mighty hot out there…'

CHAPTER FIVE

NICK told Rose everything there was to know about the time-table for his project and what had inspired him to pick Borneo for its location. Over a bottle of wine and some delivery Chinese food, which they ate in his ultra-modern, rarely used kitchen, he explained his connections with Malaysia, starting with an old university friend with whom the project was to be undertaken, and ending with an impassioned and persuasive belief that Borneo would soon be the rising star as Kuala Lumpur and Penang became overrun with tourists.

Rose did her utmost to play down her excitement and treat the whole thing as something that happened practically every day. She asked cool, sensible questions but her mind was running rampant with thoughts of planes and sea and lush green forests and, of course, being sequestered somewhere remote with him.

That was the most frightening aspect of the whole thing. How on earth was she going to maintain her sang-froid when she would be with him twenty-four seven? How long before her professional mask slipped and she made a complete fool of herself? Thus far, Nick had no idea that she followed him with her eyes, drinking in the powerful lines of his body, feasting on his harsh beauty, filing away throwaway remarks, the way he laughed, the slashing gestures he used when he was in a bad mood, so that she could bring them out at a later date and savour them like a guilty secret.

To him, she was the ugly duckling he had rescued out of obligation who, she hoped, was proving herself to be as efficient an employee as he could have asked for. Occasionally he teased her and very occasionally some of that teasing bordered on flirtation, but Rose, having lived her life in the shadow of her stunning sister, was a realist. Charming, good-looking men liked charming, good-looking women. A beautiful woman, for a man like Nick Papaeliou, was an essential accessory and if he occasionally flirted with his plain employee, then it was simply an overspill from his unconscious ability to charm. She shuddered to think how he would react if he ever found out about her inappropriately lustful imaginings.

She would be brought back down to earth by Nick listing her duties once they arrived at their destination.

Rose, who had been anxiously day-dreaming her way into a fictitious and awkward scenario in which he was roaring with laughter as he spotted her following him with puppy eyes as he dived into an imaginary swimming pool, surfaced to find him frowning.

'You are going to be able to accompany me, aren't you, Rose? You did say when I took you on that you had a valid passport.'

'Oh, yes,' Rose answered brightly.

'Because you seemed to be a million miles away just then.' He leaned towards her, eyes narrowed, and Rose automatically flinched back. 'Is there something you should tell me?' he demanded unsmilingly and for a few, disturbing seconds Rose thought that he had read her mind and exposed her shameful little secret.

'S-something I should tell you?' she stammered weakly.

'Fear of flying, maybe?' Nick leaned back and looked at her thoughtfully. 'It's nothing to be ashamed of. I know you haven't done much overseas travel…'

'Too busy touring the UK in search of spiritual zen,' Rose said, weak with relief.

'Right. But there's no need to be afraid of flying. Believe it or not, there's more chance of you ending up under the wheels of a car than plummeting from the sky.'

'Oh. Well, thank you very much for reassuring me that those great metal birds can stay airborne,' she said sarcastically, recovering her equilibrium.

'Then what's the problem?'

'I…don't have a problem, Nick.' She would have to take a swimsuit; she sure as hell wasn't going to take a bikini. She would take a very sensible one-piece and sneak out under cover of night to have a swim. The thought of frolicking in a pool with him made her feel sick.

'There you go again.'

'There I go again *what*?'

'Frowning and getting that distant look in your eyes.' He reached forward and before she was aware of his intention he smoothed her brow with his thumb. It was such an unexpected gesture that Rose literally jumped and gave a little yelp of shock.

'You're on edge. Why? If you're not scared of flying, then is it the unknown?'

'Yes.' She wanted to rub where he had touched and brush away the scorched sensation she was feeling. 'I'm scared of the unknown.'

'Thought so,' Nick said with satisfaction, 'although I can't understand why. You had a pretty nomadic existence growing up. If anything, I would have thought you would have found

he unknown quite appealing. Don't we always long to revisit
ur childhood?'

Rose had done her best to discourage any personal conversation between them. She felt safer when their relationship
was purely on a business footing. Yes, of course he asked
about the house and the work being done on it and naturally
she answered him because the house was, really and truly, the
reason why she now found herself working for him. But
beyond that, she was vague when he asked her what plans she
had for the weekend, or how she spent her evenings or even
what sort of people she met in the hotel, whether she liked
them or not.

However, she was so relieved that he had misunderstood
her apprehensive expression that she gratefully clung onto his
fear-of-the-unknown nonsense for dear life.

'Sometimes it doesn't work that way,' Rose said distantly.
She stood up and began clearing away the empty containers,
which looked a little unhealthy as the leftover contents began
to congeal.

'No?' Nick pulled a chair towards him and propped his feet
up on the black leather. After weeks of working with her, sitting
within touching range of her when they brainstormed over
some niggling problem, brushing her arm with his as he leaned
to consult architectural drawings, growing strangely accustomed to seeing her now when he came in through the front
door, he could honestly say that he still didn't know much about
her personal life. She had piqued his curiosity a long time ago
but, instead of proximity doing what it should have done, and
diminishing it, he was more curious about her than ever before.

Now she was throwing him a glimpse into her thoughts
and, like a dog tossed a bone, he was annoyed to find himself
picking it up and preparing to run with it.

'You mean you're scared of what you don't know even though you spent your formative years dealing with it?'

Rose shrugged. She had her back to him, which suited her. It helped her keep her voice steady as she spoke. 'You should be doing this, Nick. This is your house and these are your dishes.'

'But you're a woman and I'm a man. Don't women love doing things like that? Keeps them busy and happy.'

Rose spun around, but her heated accusation of sexism died on her lips when she saw the grin plastered across his face. Without thinking she flung the tea towel at him and he caught it and tut-tutted under his breath.

'I should punish you for that,' he drawled. 'Trying to cause grievous bodily harm to your employer…'

Rose felt her mouth go dry. This was the lazy, flirty voice he sometimes pulled out of the bag, with the dexterity of a magician pulling a rabbit out of a hat, and, it didn't seem to matter how many times she told herself that he was just one of those born charmers, that voice still got to her every time.

'With a tea cloth?' she said lightly. 'You must be a lot more delicate than you look if a tea cloth can inflict serious injury.' A brief, electric silence greeted this remark and Rose clenched her hands into fists behind her back. She didn't know what had possessed her to say that.

'Should I take it as a compliment that you consider me big and strong?' Nick murmured provocatively. He could tell that she would have liked the ground to open and swallow her up and for the first time since she had started working for him, he felt suddenly enraged. Enraged that he had given this woman an opportunity many would have killed for. Enraged that she continued to treat him with the studied politeness of a stranger. Enraged that every single time he had tried to get under that armour of hers, he had found himself gently but firmly repelled. Enraged now that she was back to looking at him with something like horror, as usual turning a perfectly innocent, teasing remark into something diabolical.

'Forget I said that.' Nick's voice was cool and dismissive. He even turned away.

Rose was stricken. How was he supposed to know that she shrank away from him because she was just so damn scared that if she didn't her treacherous legs would have her pelting towards him and her even more treacherous arms would wind themselves around his neck and cling?

What must he think of her? That she was ungrateful? Churlish? Buttoned up? The sort of woman who had suffered a sense-of-humour bypass somewhere along the line?

Rose wondered whether maybe she had.

'I'm sorry,' she faltered.

'What about?' Nick enquired politely.

'I'm really excited about going to Borneo…' Humourless. Buttoned up. An efficient little worker bee who actually thought that what she had to say mattered to Nick Papaeliou. He was courteous, even teasing and flirtatious sometimes, and yet here she was, lips tightly pursed, as if her maidenly honour were under threat. Clutching her precious, uninteresting private life as if one single lapse would send him into a sexual, predatory frenzy. The idea was so nonsensical that Rose inwardly cringed.

'But I guess I'm a little scared as well…'

'Oh, yes?' Nick reluctantly felt himself drawn to that simple, hesitant admission. 'Why?'

Rose sighed and went to sit at the kitchen table. She rested her chin thoughtfully in the palm of her hand and stared back down the years. She had agreed with him, initially, because he had conveniently supplied her with an excuse for her own disturbing train of thoughts, but now she thought that maybe he was right. Maybe she was scared of the unknown.

'Tony and Flora always thought that traipsing around the country would make me brave and adventurous. I think they kind of figured that some of their let's-change-the-goalposts lifestyle would rub off on me, but it never did. When you move from school to school, you end up dreading each upheaval even more than the last one. At least, that's what it did for me. It's why I like working for Fedco.'

'You can hide behind the size?' he guessed shrewdly, now fully ensnared by her dreamy, distant voice.

'I can be safe. Borneo…' Rose laughed and blinked so that he was back in her line of vision. 'Well, Borneo is just something else altogether.'

'All that heat…'

'And insects…'

Anything could happen. He nearly said it out loud and caught himself in the nick of time. 'But Tony and Flora would be pleased…'

Rose gave him a dazzling grin. 'More than pleased. They'd be overjoyed. You want to hear them on the subject of Lily. They're thrilled to bits that she's now on the other side of the world making her fortune. I think they feel that they've somehow contributed to that.'

'And what about you?'

'I would never contemplate living across the Atlantic.'

'I mean, are *you* thrilled that your sister is making her fortune on the other side of the world?'

'I've got accustomed to it,' Rose told him. 'I miss her terribly, but it helps knowing that she's happy and fulfilled.'

'And are you?'

'Am I what?'

'Happy and fulfilled.' Nick wasn't quite sure why he had asked the question. He could only think that he must be out of practice when it came to women, because experience had taught him that questions like that provoked answers he didn't like.

'Well, I'm pretty pleased with how the house is coming along.' Rose scuttled back into her shell. 'Have I told you that I'm going to have it redecorated top to bottom? The whole place is destroyed and, rather than do a patch up job, I'm going to go all the way and really have it exactly how I want it.'

'Interesting. Sounds like you're there for the long term.'

'At least for the foreseeable future,' Rose said vaguely. 'But tell me a bit more about Borneo…what else do I need to know…?'

That it took for ever to get there. That was something he hadn't told her and it was just as well as it had allowed her no opportunity to spend three days angsting over the ordeal of sitting next to him on a plane for a seemingly never-ending period of time. Rose had had enough angst on her plate just worrying about what she was going to buy to take with her.

Then there was the whole question of what exactly she was supposed to do once she got there. She might be a whizz at computers and, yes, facts, figures and financial projections were things she could handle without too much difficulty. And reporting back on her hotel, chatting to the manager, with whom she had developed a pleasant rapport, about the nuts and bolts of city chic, was within her spec…but looking at land in a country she had barely heard of and could only vaguely point to on a map?

'Okay. Spit it out.'

'What?'

'There's something on your mind. Spit it out.'

Nick snapped shut his laptop computer, sat back and gave her his full, undivided attention.

'I don't know what you mean.'

'I mean you've barely spoken since we took off four hours ago, you've been stuck on the same page of your book for the past hour and if you chew your lip any more we'll have to see if there are any paramedics on the plane. Tell me you're not worrying about what the hot weather is going to do to your hair.'

'Hardly. I stopped worrying about what my hair did years ago.'

'Relax. Enjoy the flight, as our air steward would say.' He glanced around him and then shot her a lazy, amused smile. 'Is first class all it's cracked up to be?'

Rose had had to stop herself from fidgeting with gadgets and demonstrating just how impressionable she was when it came to long-haul travel. 'And the rest,' she confessed. 'And I am very appreciative…well…for this and for…everything else…'

Nick frowned. This wasn't what he wanted to hear. Gratitude wasn't what this woman was all about. Stubborn, feisty, mutinous and often highly aggravating, yes. But grateful…no. Over the past three days, Nick had found himself looking forward to this trip. The man who had crossed the Atlantic a million times and more, who had platinum frequent-flyer cards from just about every major airline, who could afford to go anywhere in the world on a whim if he so desired, and in the company of pretty much any woman he wanted…and he had been looking forward to a business trip with a woman who made his teeth snap together in sheer frustration quite a bit of the time.

He had never been one to spend hours soul-searching, but his illogical reaction did make him conclude that his life was full of yes-men, people who would jump if he looked in their direction and silently mouthed the order.

'I don't want your thanks and gratitude,' he grated, and Rose gave him a startled glance.

'Fine,' Rose snapped back.

'So tell me what's wrong.'

'I'm not sure I'm up to what I'm supposed to do when we get to Borneo,' she admitted in a sulky voice. 'I work with computers. I don't know the first thing about building sites and conveyancing.'

'You won't have to. My Malaysian counterpart is very competent. You won't be shoved into a position where you have to make technical decisions that are beyond your scope.'

'So why am I here, in that case?'

Ah. Now, this was back to normal. Rose clambering onto her argumentative bandwagon, although her tone of voice couldn't have been more polite. He was, he had discovered, beginning to know her.

'There's more to a hotel than foundations and planning permission. Let's just say that you're here to provide the female touch.'

'Which is what exactly?'

'You argue too much.'

'Only with you.' Their eyes tangled and Rose looked away hurriedly.

'I'll take that as a compliment. It's nice to know that I can fire you up.'

Rose ground her teeth together and Nick let out a loud laugh that drew stares from the passengers sitting closest to them. 'Think about the things that impressed you most about the hotel in London, think about how they could be incorporated into a small hotel sitting in the equatorial belt. It's going to need an almighty leap of the imagination, but you know what I want…' *I want you.* The thought weaved a path in his head and he greeted it without surprise. Maybe he had known all along that she was more than just a challenge or a novelty or a refreshing break from the type of women he usually enjoyed. He wanted her. Not just her mind, but her body. Nick lowered his eyes.

Every inch of him gave the impression of a man totally absorbed by what his companion was saying. She certainly seemed to have taken on board everything he had told her in the past about his plans, even things he had mentioned in passing. Now, enthused, she was eagerly discussing them and he made sure to contribute, but the flicker of his eyes was on her mouth, soft and pink, and her breasts, shadowy outlines under her cotton pinstriped shirt as she leant towards him, her hands articulating what she was saying. Something about sunken baths and a rainforest decor that would bring the environment right into the hotel.

'I did think about buying a guidebook,' she finished, 'but I wanted to be assaulted by the place without any preconceived ideas.'

'Yes. Good idea.' Nick smiled, setting her at ease. 'Right…now let's compare some of those preliminary costings…'

How could she ever have thought that a life devoid of change and adventure was a good one?

Here she was, sitting in the first-class compartment of a plane that would deliver her first to Kuala Lumpur and then onward to Kota Kinabalu, the state capital of Sabah, places she had never heard of in her life before. And, yes, it was exciting.

She looked at Nick surreptitiously from under her lashes and felt that familiar illicit thrill. He was sleeping, his body half inclined away from her so that all she could glimpse was his profile and the gentle rise and fall of his chest.

The seats in first class could be extended to full body length and, although she was as reclined as he was and the cabin was in darkness, she was finding it difficult to sleep.

For the first time, she could sort of understand how Tony and Flora had been affected by wanderlust. The unknown wasn't scary, as she had imagined. Or rather, she amended to herself, it was scary, but it was also full of possibilities.

The strongest possibility now was that she would remain wide awake for the remainder of the trip and then be fit for nothing when they eventually landed.

But she slept.

And the next few hours so completely removed her from everything that was familiar to her that Rose, delighted and disoriented, put herself firmly in Nick's care. Connections were made, passports were checked and she just looked around her open-mouthed, until finally they were on the last stage of their travel, quickly covering the two-and-a-half hour trip towards Kota Kinabalu.

Daylight was already fading by the time they were being delivered to their hotel, but it was still very, very hot.

'It's…not what I expected…'

'You can hardly keep your eyes open, Rose. As soon as we get to the hotel, you can climb into your bed and fall asleep. Don't try and appreciate the scenery now.'

'But how is it I feel sleepy and you don't?'

'I'm an experienced traveller.' He gave her an amused, mocking glance.

The taxi swung round a corner and there, following a long drive through manicured lawns, was the hotel. As she stepped out of the taxi she was aware of a thousand tiny night sounds.

'I'm aiming for something more eco-friendly than this,' Nick murmured into her ear. 'It's big but, in terms of comfort, you'll be hard pressed to better it. Now, I shall get us checked in and then you're going to go to your room and get some sleep.'

'I wish I'd read that guidebook after all.' She yawned ruefully.

'No need. Lee Peng knows this place like the back of his hand. A living guide is a damn sight better than someone else's interpretation of a place.'

'I feel awful leaving you to go to bed…don't think that I won't be pulling my weight…perhaps if I just freshen up a bit, I could join you and we could go over plans for tomorrow…'

Nick ignored her valiant protests and checked them in while Rose loitered behind him, savouring the glassy marble flooring and the cool, colonial elegance of the foyer. Were these the perks of working for a rich man? Everything done in style, with no expense spared.

She was shown to her quarters by one of the smiling porters and only when the door closed behind her did she realise how tired she really was.

She closed her eyes on a bedroom that was all ceiling fans and bamboo blinds and soft mosquito nets and rattan furniture, and a bathroom that she would have to devote some time to in the morning as she spied the sunken bath.

And awoke abruptly, it seemed like five minutes later, to the sound of tapping from behind the blinds she had hurriedly pulled down earlier.

When Rose looked at her watch, she saw to her horror that it was already eight-thirty. She had slept for nearly ten hours. And for the first time in weeks her internal alarm system had not woken her up at three in the morning for no better reason than to fill her head with thoughts she didn't want.

The tapping on the door galvanised her into action. It was probably the cleaning service making her feel like a lazy slob instead of the working woman she was supposed to be. She wasn't sure what room Nick was in, but she would have to get through to him immediately through the operator and assure him in her crispest voice that she would be ready to start work in fifteen minutes.

No need. Rose pulled up the exquisite bamboo blinds and there he was, standing outside what was, in fact, a glass door that she could now see led to a small wooden patio, along one side of which was a hammock, next to a couple of chairs and a small table, all perfect for relaxing outside and gazing at the scenery. In this case, lush lawns liberally interspersed with coconut trees, which led down to a beach. To the left, she could glimpse the pool, just a slash of bright blue surrounded by turquoise umbrellas and yet more coconut trees in between.

But she took all this in in literally a couple of seconds.

As she had discovered, nothing could compete for her attention when Nick was in the vicinity.

'It's you.' Where was her crisp voice when she needed it? Suddenly conscious of the fact that she was still in just her nightie and the thin bathrobe she had flung on before leaping towards the door in a surge of guilt for having overslept, Rose folded her arms and tried to look composed.

'Who did you think it was going to be?'

'The cleaning service. I…I…was actually just about to phone through to you and let you know that I'll be ready to start work shortly.'

'No need to phone.' Nick gave a slight inclination of his head. 'I'm in the cabin next to yours. In fact, if you go around that flimsy wooden lattice partition, you'll be at my glass door…' He had seen her in many guises, from angry to embarrassed to primly correct, but he had never seen her like this, flushed from sleep, her skin satin-smooth, hair tousled.

Nick made no apologies to himself for wanting her. He had

recognised that kick of desire and his sole objective now was to sate it. Had she been his full-time employee, he would have done his damnedest to shut the door firmly on all thoughts of seduction, but fortunately she wasn't.

Rose tried not to look horrified at this piece of information. 'I'm sure that won't be necessary. If you want to give me fifteen minutes, Nick, I'll join you in the foyer.'

'No need to be so formal.' He leaned against the frame of the sliding patio door. 'I've ordered breakfast to be brought to my room for both of us. When you're ready, just skip across. Continental all right for you? Oh, and I thought we might as well appreciate the surroundings today. Enjoy the beach, see what the poolside facilities are…we can start in earnest tomorrow when Lee's back from KL.'

Several things he had just said converged to send her into a state of mild panic. Sharing breakfast. In his room. Enjoying the facilities.

Rose cleared her throat, wondering how she could pick her way through her objections and emerge on the other side without appearing to overreact, but he was already turning away, only glancing back to give her a nonchalant wave.

She had brought no clothes to cover breakfast with her sexy boss in his room. He had been wearing a pair of khaki Bermuda shorts and a collared tee shirt. In between the confusion of what he had been saying to her, she had managed to notice the elegant, casual ease with which he pulled off an outfit that most men would have looked frightful in.

Rose rummaged through her bags at the speed of light and tried to block out the image of his legs, bronzed and muscular, sprinkled with dark hair.

Was he hairy all over? she wondered feverishly.

Yet another thought to try and dispel as she flung on a

Get FREE BOOKS and FREE GIFTS when you play the...

LAS VEGAS GAME

Just scratch off the gold box with a coin. Then check below to see the gifts you get!

YES! I have scratched off the gold box. Please send me my **2 FREE BOOKS** and **2 FREE GIFTS** for which I qualify. I understand that I am under no obligation to purchase any books as explained on the back of this card.

306 HDL ENUG   106 HDL ENZG

FIRST NAME   LAST NAME

ADDRESS

APT.#   CITY

STATE/PROV.   ZIP/POSTAL CODE   (H-P-03/08)

7	7	7	Worth TWO FREE BOOKS plus TWO BONUS Mystery Gifts!
			Worth TWO FREE BOOKS!
			TRY AGAIN!

www.eHarlequin.com

Offer limited to one per household and not valid to current subscribers of Harlequin Presents®. All orders subject to approval.

Your Privacy - Harlequin Books is committed to protecting your privacy. Our privacy policy is available online at www.eHarlequin.com or upon request from the Harlequin Reader Service. From time to time we make our lists of customers available to reputable third parties who may have a product or service of interest to you. If you would prefer for us not to share your name and address, please check here. ☐

▼ DETACH AND MAIL CARD TODAY! ▼

© 2007 HARLEQUIN ENTERPRISES LTD. ® and ™ are trademarks owned and used by the trademark owner and/or its licensee.

If offer card is missing write to: Harlequin Reader Service, 3010 Walden Ave., P.O. Box 1867, Buffalo, NY 14240-1867

BUSINESS REPLY MAIL
FIRST-CLASS MAIL   PERMIT NO. 717   BUFFALO, NY

POSTAGE WILL BE PAID BY ADDRESSEE

HARLEQUIN READER SERVICE
3010 WALDEN AVE
PO BOX 1867
BUFFALO NY 14240-9952

NO POSTAGE
NECESSARY
IF MAILED
IN THE
UNITED STATES

baggy tee shirt, all the better to hide her figure, and a pair of trousers that would probably reduce her to a puddle of perspiration by the middle of the day but which would have to do. At least until she gained a little colour and her confidence grew.

She arrived, flustered, to find him sitting on his veranda sipping a cup of coffee, legs stretched out on one of the chairs, leaving her to sit closer to him than she had bargained for.

'Gorgeous, isn't it?' was the first thing he said as she sat down and poured herself some orange juice. She could feel her heart beating madly in her chest.

'Stunning.'

He slid his eyes over to where she was staring pointedly away from him and across to the pool area. 'You really shouldn't wear trousers, Rose. Too hot.'

'I…I haven't unpacked as yet. I just grabbed these from the top of the suitcase.'

'Well, no matter. I suggest we take to the beach after this so you'll have to change into a swimsuit anyway. We can get whatever beach towels we need from Reception.' Nick relished the thought of seeing her in a swimsuit. It was hard to get any idea of her shape under the loose-fitting clothes she seemed to favour and he fancied she was more curvy than the magazines currently deemed fashionable.

'But aren't we here to…work?' Rose asked desperately. She crumbled a croissant in half as he did the same and tried to focus nonchalantly on the fact that he would have seen thousands of women in swimsuits. He wouldn't look twice at her.

'Lateral thinking.' Nick demolished one half of his croissant in a single bite and wiped his mouth with his serviette. The breeze was light and warm and very, very inviting. Yes, work was on the agenda, but he had to admit to himself that he felt very relaxed, more relaxed than he had in years.

'Lateral thinking,' Rose repeated and he nodded sagely at her.

'We have a few possible locations to have a look at and we'll do that tomorrow with Lee, but basically the rest of the time here will be…investigative work…'

'I thought we had meetings lined up. Don't we have to go over plans with your architects? What about the buildings inspector?' She had envisaged days packed with meetings and the gritty business of getting the ball rolling on foreign soil. Of course, they might share the occasional meal together, but on the hop so to speak. And he knew people in the area. Evenings, she had reckoned, he would spend with them, catching up on old times. It was what any normal human being would do.

Investigative work did not fit into her overall picture of their ten days on the island.

'There's a hell of a lot to see here. Coffee? Another croissant? Yes, as I was saying, there's a lot to see.' He relaxed back and clasped his hands together behind his head. 'Did you know, for example, that Borneo is the world's third largest island? That Sabah, the proposed site for my venture, has some of the oldest rainforests in the world? Oh, yes. There's a lot more to this place than the beach you see down there…and naturally, we have to check it all out so that we can decide where the ideal location would be. Beach or forest? Should we cater for the lazy traveller or the adventurous one? One person may be content to sit in the sun by a pool or stroll down to the beach and while away the day in a deckchair with a constant supply of cocktails on tap. Another may want to trek through the jungle in search of an orang-utan or two. Did you know that over here the orang-utan is known as the "wild man of Borneo"?'

'We're going to see orang-utans?'

'Not until we've checked out that pool and, of course, the beach.' He stood up and stretched, then stuck his hands in his pockets and stared out towards the sea. 'Fascinating place this…where else can you find rainforests and white beaches sharing the same space? You'll see for yourself, but all in good time. For now…' he nodded towards the beach '…a lazy day checking out the competition.'

And sitting in front of a lukewarm cup of coffee and a half-eaten croissant was no longer an option. It was a glorious day, the sun was hot and she had absolutely no excuse to wriggle out of a swim in the sea.

Anyway, Nick's suggestions were often thinly veiled commands. And she was being paid generously by him. Some might well say that being paid to swim in the clear South China Sea was a pretty good deal.

Rose wasn't precisely thinking along those lines as she flung clothes hurriedly into drawers while deciding which of her three black swimsuits she would wear. She was thinking that there was safety in nursing her attraction under the respectable cloak of their professional relationship. Even if that professional relationship was a little more unorthodox than most. Indeed, the fact that she worked for him in his house probably accounted for her inconvenient attraction. Made sense. After all, she had previously felt exactly the opposite sentiment before she had found herself cooped up under his roof.

She had a brief feeling of triumph, as though she had managed to solve a complex maths problem.

Then she looked at herself in the long standing mirror by the wall. As swimsuits went, this one was modest. But yet there was cleavage to be seen, far too much for her liking, and legs and shoulders and the generous proportions that always made her want to cringe…

And on a beach…with his body on display…not just
snatched glimpses of bare chest where the top two buttons of
his shirt were undone…where was her protection going to be?

CHAPTER SIX

THE beach was uncrowded. Too early, Rose guessed, for most of the guests. The same large canopied umbrellas that adorned the sides of the pool were in evidence along the beach, dotted here and there, and closer to the glassy, lake-like sea similar-coloured padded deckchairs were interspersed. Further along, she could see that a thin finger of land projected into the sea and from a distance might have passed for a jetty were it not for the coconut trees growing along it.

It was a breathtaking sight. Really a vision of paradise, from the white powdery sand dappled with shadows cast by the overhanging coconut trees, to the still, dazzling azure of the sea.

Rose paused and savoured the scene through the protective lenses of her very dark sunglasses. She had decided to maintain her inclination to conceal her shape by wearing a knee-length, flimsy beach dress and she could already feel the rising sun burning through it.

Along the beach, a couple of the deckchairs were occupied by early risers who were mostly reading and wearing sensible large straw hats.

Typically, Nick was nowhere to be seen and Rose was

peering into the distance when she felt a hand on her shoulder and he said, with a thread of amusement in his voice, 'Why are you wearing a sheet?'

Rose swung around and glared at him from behind her sunglasses. 'I'm trying to protect myself from the sun,' she snapped. 'It's fine for you. You can tan easily but I'm a lot fairer. In fact, coming out into the sun at this hour is not a very good idea at all for someone of my complexion.'

Which, she admitted to herself, was something of a slight overstatement given it was still quite early in the day.

He, of course, was bare-backed but for the towel swung casually over his shoulders. As promised, he had brought hers with him and he reached out to give it to her, still grinning.

'You should have brought a sombrero with you…like those practical people further along.'

Rose snatched the towel and began walking away, but slowed down at the notion that he might be sniggering as he watched her wobbly, none-too-toned rear.

She took heart from the comforting thought that this was not a holiday, this was work.

They seemed to be walking away from the scattering of people on the beach and she immediately set that particular situation right by heading towards one of the lounging chairs not far from an elderly lady who was napping with her book over her face.

'Are you going to remove that garment of yours? Because I warn you—the sun here is very hot. Much hotter than in England.'

'I've brought a notebook. I thought we might start jotting down a few things in connection with work.' She felt pleasantly secure behind the sunglasses and half watched as he spread his towel on the sand, ignoring the sun lounger, and lay flat on it. As if that weren't distracting enough, he began to rub sun cream haphazardly over his body.

'Even I burn,' he assured her. He could feel her watching him. She did that. Watched him. Nick was used to women watching him, but the concealed way she did it had become a powerful turn-on. He wanted her, but he wasn't going to get her through outrageous flirting or expensive gifts. He settled back, closed his eyes and waited for the prolonged silence to have the desired effect.

Eventually, Rose spoke, keeping her treacherous eyes away from the tempting sight of his practically naked, bronzed body. 'What made you decide to go into…well…hotels?'

'You sound like an interviewer.'

'It's only polite curiosity,' Rose said. 'Everyone has a reason for doing what they do.'

'And you went into computing because…?'

'We're not discussing me.' The sun was beginning to make her feel lazy and peaceful. She didn't want an argument. She wanted to close her eyes and let her chattering thoughts slip away. 'I bet you don't even stay in many hotels.'

'On the contrary. I'm rarely out of them.'

'I meant for pleasure as opposed to business.' She glanced down at him and realised that he was barely listening to her. His eyes were closed and she was pretty sure that his thoughts were a million miles away. She carefully inched the flimsy beach robe off and began applying a generous layer of sunblock to her exposed skin, keeping a careful eye on him because lying flat she felt a whole lot more confident about her body than when she was sitting up, where her stomach, smooth as it might be, still seemed to have the last laugh at her for having spent years guiltily avoiding the gym.

Or maybe she was simply comparing herself to Lily who

had a washboard abdomen even when she was slouching and breathing out.

Job done, Rose lay back down and shaded her face with the magazine she had brought from her room.

'Hotels for pleasure…hmm…well, maybe it's the pull of the challenge, to boldly embark on a project of which I have zero experience. There's nothing like the possibility of failure to get the adrenaline going.'

She was aware that he had half turned towards her and she kept her eyes firmly shielded behind her magazine.

'I've conquered the money markets,' Nick said casually. 'Or rather, I've made enough money to live comfortably for the rest of my life, even if I decided never to lift a finger again. Very comfortably. What does a man do when he reaches that position?'

'Retire and enjoy what life has to offer,' Rose said, surprised. 'But then, who would you enjoy it with?'

Nick sat up and lifted the magazine from her face, which immediately brought her shooting up so that they were staring at each other fully.

'Sorry,' she mumbled. 'That remark just sort of slipped out.'

'Working with computers, Rose, might not have been the best career move for you.'

'Meaning?'

'Meaning you have no tact.' Nick would have left any other woman in no doubt that overstepping the boundaries was tantamount to a still-born relationship. However there was, he reminded himself, no relationship with this woman and, anyway, she was already bristling. Of course, he wasn't about to back down and allow a woman, any woman, to invade his private space, but was he really ready for a fight? When the sun was beating down on his back and the sea glimmered invitingly?

'You mean that sometimes I don't agree with you.'

'I'm going for a swim.' Nick stood up, a profile of one-hundred-per-cent masculine beauty, and glanced back over his shoulder to her. 'Coming?'

'I think I'll just stay here, thanks, and carry on sunbathing,' Rose flounced back onto her lounger and stuck the magazine back into position.

The notebook that she had packed to remind herself that work was the reason for her lazing on a lounger on a beach remained unopened in her bag. She had a moment of brief despair as she contemplated the remainder of their stay, then she turned her thoughts to his high-handed attitude, telling her she was lacking tact. It felt a lot better to fulminate.

By the time she had worked herself up some healthy self-righteous anger, the sun was beginning its ascent and pleasantly warm was turning into baking hot.

Rose reluctantly shelved her thoughts, sat up and glanced at her watch to discover, with shock, that Nick had now been swimming for over forty minutes, and when she peered towards the horizon, there was no sign of him.

Panic slammed into her and she shot to her feet and hurried down to the water line, shielding her eyes from the glare of the sun. The beach was more crowded now, although still relatively deserted. People were in the water. A quick glance told her that Nick was not among their number.

She obeyed her instinct and forged into the sea, which was so warm that her body barely needed to adjust to the temperature.

The one continuity in her life had been her swimming lessons. Tony and Flora had nurtured a vague, hippie-like notion that swimming was akin to being at one with nature, and, with that in mind, they had insisted on swimming lessons wherever they had happened to be. The Education of Life was more important than the education of the classroom, but swimming was something they had insisted upon. And Rose had enjoyed it so much that she had continued even when classes had no longer been necessary and long after Lily had packed it in because it ruined her hair. Rose, never one to spend time agonising over the state of her hair, had found the silence and privacy of swimming a soothing balm to a tumultuous adolescence.

Feeling the water on her was like coming home.

As she struck out she wondered whether she should have run further up the beach in search of a lifeguard, but the thought of creating a scene, probably for no reason, was offputting, never mind Nick's reaction if he returned from a simple swim to find the hotel's rescue party hot on his trail.

Anyway, it was too late to think about that.

She was pretty sure she would spot him a little further out, and then she could slink back to shore, safe in the knowledge that he was all right.

She swam confidently out but then, when the beach was beginning to look a little too distant for the sake of comfort, she felt the slow crawl of fear through her because who knew what inhabited the waters? They looked crystal-clear and perfectly innocent, but anything could be lurking in the depths. What if he had been sucked under by something? Were box jellyfish rampant in these waters or was she mixing up her oceans?

That thought was enough to convince her that heading back to shore and summoning the search party was the best course of action.

She was hardly aware of the shape quickly gaining on her until she felt something on her waist and she spluttered in sharp, sudden panic to a stop.

'Were you worried?' Nick was laughing as he edged back from her.

Relief turned to anger and she glared at him, tempted to hit him smartly on his sexy, grinning face, but her training kicked in. Any kind of tussle in water was a bad idea.

'I was hot,' she snarled, turning away and beginning to strike out back for land.

He caught her again, this time by her ankle, and she spun around and began treading water. 'In case you don't know,' she snapped, 'it's dangerous to fight in the water.'

'Who's fighting?' He flicked his head in the direction of the promontory she had noticed earlier on. 'In case you were wondering how come you couldn't find me…I was on that strip of land. I saw you swimming out and decided to meet you.'

'Just in case I ran into problems?'

'Can't have my employee drowning on my watch, can I?'

'I happen to be a very strong swimmer.'

'I noticed.'

Rose wasn't sure that she liked the thought of him looking at her while she had been swimming.

'So…joining me? We could always swim back to shore and walk across, but better exercise this way.'

She didn't think he needed the exercise. Unlike her. But she was enjoying the water and she suddenly wanted to prove just how good a swimmer she was. She nodded and then headed strongly away towards the strip of land, invigorated as he swam up behind her, then alongside and finally in front, easily making it to land before her so that she found herself coming out of the water, dripping wet, with no protective outer layer of baggy clothing, while he sat on the sand and surveyed her at his leisure.

Self-consciousness kicked in along with all the insecurities she had always had about her body, ones which should have been put to bed a long time ago because, really, what did looks matter?

Everything about her was unfashionably big. Her breasts were not the pert, small bumps beloved by fashionistas, her hair was too uncontrollable, her frame was just too short and stocky and she was sure that her rear could have done with several thousand more trips to the local swimming pool.

And there he was. A study in casual male beauty, sitting lazily on the trunk of a fallen coconut tree.

Her modest swimsuit suddenly felt like a handkerchief tied together with a few bits of string and Rose wrapped her arms around her body in a show of feeling cold.

'I really never thought that this would be part of a working trip over here,' she said crossly, all too aware that he was sizing her up and finding her wanting in every department.

She had, he noticed, made sure to sit as far away from him as was humanly possible without it looking glaringly obvious. Coy, he thought, not for the first time, was not a word in her vocabulary. Neither were the words flirting or teasing. If she had had her notebook to hand, he was pretty certain that she would have brandished it just to make sure that he got her hands-off message.

Once upon a time, he might have been amused by that because his hands would not have wanted to be on her, but not so now.

Next to her, the women he had dated in the past were stick insects, devoid of personality and sex appeal. He wanted to tell her that instead of huddling next to him, arms wrapped around her body in an attempt to hide the glorious abundance of her body, she should revel in her womanly curves.

However he acknowledged that she would probably hit

him if he did that, so he dragged his eyes reluctantly away from her and resigned himself to the prospect of a slow seduction via harmless small talk, not a route he had ever favoured.

'What do you think of this spot?'

Rose inwardly breathed a sigh of relief. She had been half expecting something sarcastic along the lines of her resemblance to a beached whale. Scenery, she figured, she could expound upon, and she did, asking him a million questions about Borneo. Whenever there appeared to be a pause in the conversation, in she jumped to carry on the subject while the sun continued to rise in the sky. Eventually, Nick turned to her and raised his eyebrows.

'So, do you think we have exhausted the tourist angle?'

'I'm interested.'

'You're sunburnt.'

'What?' Rose automatically raised her hands to her face, allowing Nick a bird's-eye view of her luscious breasts, which her severely cut swimsuit was having a hard time concealing.

'Right there.' He ran his finger quickly along the strip of her nose and Rose pulled back with a little yelp of shock. 'We need to get you back to our towels and bags.'

'Oh, no. I've only just thought—were they safe being left on the beach?'

'As houses.' Nick stood up and held out his hand for her to take.

Flustered, Rose grasped it and he pulled her neatly to her feet, covertly watching her breasts bounce as she gathered her balance. Since when, he wondered, had he become a dirty old man, covertly watching a woman's body and getting turned on?

'You never did tell me…' Rose said as they strolled back towards their possessions, which, as he had predicted, were exactly where they had been left.

'What?' Nick enquired, staring straight ahead of him and trying to subdue his overactive imagination.

'Why you chose to branch out into the hotel business. You said that you no longer felt challenged by making money, but why hotels?'

'You mean considering I'm a sad and lonely old man still searching for the perfect woman?'

'I never said you were sad and lonely,' Rose objected, flushing.

'Just someone who had no experience of staying in a hotel for fun, an all-work-and-no-play kind of guy…'

'I'm sure you have lots of fun,' Rose stumbled, wondering how they had managed to swim out of safe waters into the perilous seas of personal conversation. It wouldn't bother him, she was certain, but it bothered her.

'Had,' Nick amended guilelessly. 'I haven't actually been out with a woman since I met your sister…'

For a few seconds Rose felt completely disoriented by that admission. He had told her that his relationship with Lily had been platonic and she had believed him. She hadn't stopped to wonder whether that had not been of his choosing and, at the thought that he might actually fancy her sister, she felt a sudden coldness in the pit of her stomach.

'Lily has been known to have that effect on men,' she said brightly, clearing her throat.

'What effect is that?'

Rose shrugged. 'Being worshipped from afar.'

'Whoever mentioned anything about worshipping her from afar?' Nick asked incredulously. 'I meant, my darling, that the night I met your sister happened to be the night I broke up with a woman and ever since then I've stayed away from the fair sex. All men need a break from complications.'

Had he just called her 'my darling'? Well, yes, not as an endearment, but for a few wild seconds her heart soared, then she registered the rest of his sentence and realised that, for whatever reason, he had decided to fill her in on a slice of his private life. He was practising celibacy.

'They do,' Rose said approvingly. 'And it's a mistake to think that sex is the answer to everything.'

Nick felt a kick of satisfaction that he had manoeuvred the conversation exactly where he wanted it. Sex. Such a small word to cover such a massive subject and, with testosterone coursing through his body, he was in the perfect mood to talk about it.

'But that's not why we're here, is it?' Rose hastened on. 'We're here to do some groundwork for your project. It doesn't matter why you wanted to go into the hotel business. That's your private matter and I know you'll agree that we shouldn't let chit-chat about our private lives intrude on the reason why we're here in the first place.' Rose felt quite proud of the adult manner in which she had grounded their wayward conversation.

One step forward, two steps backward. Nick ground his teeth together in frustration.

'Would you like me to make a list of the usual tourist sites?' Her beach dress beckoned like manna from heaven and Rose gratefully snatched it up and slipped it over her head.

'That won't be necessary, Rose.' Interesting, this feeling of having the rug pulled very swiftly out from under your feet. Interesting and not particularly agreeable. 'I suggest we use the rest of the day to do a bit of sightseeing.'

Rainforests…mountains and waterfalls…rare flora and fauna…the world-famous orang-utan sanctuary… Then a flurry of meetings and, of course, Lee Peng and his family with their abundant hospitality…supper to meet family and friends…

There was hardly time to draw breath and no time at all with Rose. Just that one morning on the beach, which, after nearly five days, seemed like a lifetime ago.

Nick had never met a woman more adroit at standing a mere five feet away from him and yet scrupulously avoiding his company. She was awash with good ideas, all faithfully detailed in her ever-present notebook and all related with an air of earnest professionalism, whenever she happened to find herself alone with him. Nightcaps at the hotel were politely but firmly rejected, with convincing yawns to back up her claims that the heat made her tired. Breakfast was always sent to her room because, and this she had told him with an apologetic smile, she liked to use the time to multitask. Eat and communicate with her friends back home via email.

With increasing frustration, Nick realised that he was gradually being reduced to the level of a schoolboy, unable to stop sneaking looks at her in her tee shirts and shorts and then fantasising about her late at night when he lay in bed staring at the ceiling and telling himself that he was behaving like a lunatic.

He could have anyone and yet when he tried to think of the many women he could have, he found his thoughts blurring and finally there she was, in his head yet again.

And here he was now. Facing another night of frustration because Rose had retired early, this time claiming the perennial headache excuse.

He looked at his watch and discovered that it was after midnight. One fifteen, to be precise, and he considered his options. Remain in bed, scowling into the darkness, or else get up and at least solve one of his problems by having a very cold shower.

He slid out from under the covers and felt the pleasantly

cool touch of tiles under his bare feet. Overhead, the fan whirred rhythmically, drowning out the little noises of night creatures outside. The prospect of a cold shower was about as appealing as the thought of switching on his computer and catching up on work, which was usually his routine when he couldn't sleep.

Nick moved quietly, without bothering to switch the lights on, and stuck on some drawstring cotton trousers, which were the closest thing to pyjama bottoms he possessed.

Making very little noise, he opened the sliding door that led onto his private veranda, from which the landscaped gardens stretched before him as a series of darkened shapes.

Borneo was proving to be a marvel of surprises. Few places, he thought, could provide such a winning combination of white sandy beaches, blue, calm sea and the spectacle that was the wonder of the rainforest.

Out of the corner of his eye, he saw something move. It was just a flicker behind the trellis separating his veranda from his neighbour's. In this instance, Rose. Normally, the leafy fronds clambering over the wooden trellis acted as a very successful screen, but in the inky blackness of the night whatever she was wearing must have been of a light colour.

Nick felt a rush of adrenaline surge through him. Without pausing to think, just acting with the unerring instincts of the predator, he circled the patch of lawn and appeared in front of her, bare backed because the night was balmy but, other than that, decently clad, if lacking shoes.

'Well, well, well,' he drawled, 'come here often?' He sprinted up the two wooden steps, not giving her time to beat a hasty retreat.

Whatever she was wearing, it was obvious she had not dressed for an accidental meeting with her boss. Her nightie

was ultra thin and barely skirted her thighs. The light trick-
ling from the room behind her was her cruellest enemy
because it showed the full, rounded outline of her bare breasts.
With a little leap of the imagination, Nick could almost see
the shape of her nipples.

Rose looked at him in horror. 'What the hell do you think
you're doing here?' she demanded, too shocked by his sudden
appearance to even think of what she was wearing.

'Same as you. Couldn't sleep.' Ever one to take full advantage of the opportunities presented to him, Nick sat on the
chair next to her and grinned. 'I know why I couldn't sleep,
but what about you?'

Rose was literally lost for words. Never in a million years
had she expected this. She could have wept with frustration
because she had done so well over the past few days. She had
behaved with impeccable and detached politeness and pointedly ignored him whenever she could get away with it, and
when she couldn't she had fallen back on talking about work.
Yes, it was an ordeal, but at least the nights were hers. And
now... How dared he invade her down time? Behaving for all
the world as though he had every right?

'I think you should go,' Rose said coldly, rising to her feet.
She snatched up the glass of water she had brought outside
with her and spun round on her heel.

'Not so fast.'

Before she knew it, he was standing in front of her, his hand
biting into her arm.

'What are you doing? Let me go.'

'Tell me why you're running away from me.'

'I am not running away from you.' If only she could sound
a bit more convincing, but her voice was a high whisper and,
Lord, her legs were like jelly.

'You mean you've suddenly and coincidentally realised that you're very tired and need to go to bed immediately?'

'I mean…' She took a deep breath to steady herself. This situation felt so intimate. Just the two of them, eyes locked, while the rest of the world slept. His semi nudity was an affront to all her senses, filling her up until it seemed to be the only thing she could see even though she was making every effort not to. 'I mean that this is my private time and I don't want you in it. I may work for you, Nick, but when I'm in my own quarters I don't really expect you to barge in as though you own the place.'

'Hardly barging in. I saw you through the trellis and, as neither of us could sleep, I figured I might as well pop over, make sure you were okay.'

'I'm fine.'

'You don't look fine. You're shaking. Are you cold? You're wearing next to nothing.'

'I'm wearing more than you.'

Nick gave her a rueful smile. 'Apologies, but like you I didn't expect company at one thirty in the morning. It was either this or nothing.'

Rose gulped.

'I don't possess pyjamas.'

'Everyone possesses pyjamas.'

'I challenge you to rifle through my belongings.'

'I beg your pardon?'

'Let's go inside. We wouldn't want the neighbours talking, would we?' There was no chance of that. The hotel was cleverly designed to ensure that guests had almost total privacy, with only the double cabanas sharing the same veranda split by leafy trellises. Nick took advantage of her momentary lapse in concentration to walk into her rooms, which were identical to his with only variations in some of the decor to differentiate the two.

She was as neat as he had expected her to be. The little sitting area was tidy, unlike his, which always bore the signs of work in progress. She had only switched on the side light by the sofa and he preferred to leave it that way.

Looking at her, he could tell that she was on the verge of imploding and it had obviously hit home that she was in a very transparent item of clothing because her arms were once more protectively around her as she hovered by the door. Wondering, no doubt, what tactic she could employ to chuck him out.

Well, he had waited for days in a state of frustration. He wasn't going to blow this chance. He wanted her and he knew that all he needed to do was smash through her veneer of polite aloofness and she would be his because she wanted him too. The air between them had sizzled ever since they had arrived on the island. He intended to douse it.

'It's mad to be up at this hour.' Rose laughed nervously, keeping her distance. 'We'll be fit for nothing in the morning and we've another busy day ahead.'

Nick strolled lazily towards her until he was standing right in front of her. In the muted light, breathtakingly sexy and very, very dangerous. Every alarm bell in her head was clamouring, but there was still a part of her that scoffed at the notion that there might be anything to be afraid of. After all, what was he going to do? A man like that? Kiss her? Men like that, she knew, made passes at girls like her sister. They didn't look at her twice and if her heart was beating like a hammer, it was simply because she was scared of her own reaction to *him*, scared of him getting physically any closer just in case her legs gave way and she did something undignified like swoon.

'Sometimes mad can be fun,' Nick mused. 'Have you never done anything mad in your life, Rose?'

'No.' Rose laughed, this time a little hysterically. 'No—' she cleared her throat and tried to get a grip '—mad really isn't me.'

'How do you know if you've never tried?'

She had managed to somehow find herself with her back to the wall, which turned out to be not a very good idea as he now laid his hands on either side of her so that she seemed to be surrounded by him, locked in and deprived, if not literally of oxygen, then certainly of the ability to think coherently.

'Here we are, Rose…on one of the most stunningly beautiful islands in the world. Outside, the night is like black velvet and in here…well, just the two of us… Shall I tell you what my mad thought is?'

No! Her head screamed. 'What?'

'This…' Nick leant into her. She felt his hand cradle the back of her neck and she almost couldn't believe what was happening even as her skin burned where he touched her.

'No…' she protested in a pathetically weak little voice and Nick half smiled, already hearing her submission and knowing, in that instant, that his suspicions had been right: she wanted him just as much as he wanted her. His body reared up with a sudden, savage heat that shocked him, and he brought his mouth down to hers, turned on by her small whimper as she parted her lips and closed her eyes.

Rose pressed her hands against his chest and felt the hard bunch of his muscles under the flat of her hand. Yes, of course she should push him away. That was a given.

She ran her hands over his chest, contouring the outline of his flat brown nipples, and moaned softly under her breath while his mouth continued to devour hers, catapulting common sense into orbit.

When she finally surfaced sufficiently to draw breath and speak, she did manage a weak protest, but her breasts, pressed against him, were aching and sensitive. Weeks of yearning left her helpless. The feel of him was like a miracle of revelation.

What had she ever done before? Had safe relationships and not even very many of them. She had chosen boyfriends on all the right grounds: compatibility, kindness, friendship.

This man was neither compatible, kind nor her friend and, even if she weren't sharp enough to have sussed that for herself, his background spoke volumes. A life strewn with women who had stepped off the front covers of magazines, dismissive of commitment, driven but for reasons she had never valued.

Nick drew back and looked down at her. 'One last chance,' he said thickly.

'For what?' She knew exactly what he was talking about.

'For decision-making. When morning comes, I don't want to be accused of taking advantage of you.'

'I would never do that.'

'You misunderstand. We both go to your bedroom with our eyes wide open or tell me now to leave.' And what would he do? Nick thought. Have another cold shower? Go for a swim in the sea? Switch on his computer and hope that numbers, reports and figures would distract him from the thought of her separated by the thickness of a wall?

He had never been in this position before, at the mercy of a woman, and he had to restrain himself from the indignity of trying to persuade her into the decision he wanted her to make.

Rose felt his body hard against hers. What choice did she have? Common sense was a plane-flight away. For now…it was time to be mad.

CHAPTER SEVEN

THIS was as overwhelming as the first fantasies of a teenage boy, although Nick was careful not to mention that to Rose. His body didn't fail to remind him of the fact, though, as he led her into the bedroom and onto the wide, king-sized bed, still rumpled from where she had been lying, with a gap in the mosquito net through which she had slipped out, presumably on her way to the veranda.

His loose cotton trousers couldn't begin to hide the urgency of his erection, but he was going to take his time, make love to her slowly and thoroughly.

'Are you sure about this?' He parted the mosquito net and looked to where she was sitting primly on the side of the bed.

'Yes, you're right. Everyone needs a little madness in their lives now and again.'

'In which case, why do you look scared to death?'

Rose flushed and looked away quickly. 'Do I?'

Nick, on the verge of slipping off the trousers, hesitated and then joined her on the bed, pulling the mosquito net behind him so that they were now enclosed in a little cocoon of their own. He might have, in the past, made the usual traditionally romantic gestures, sent the flowers, bought the expensive meals and the expensive tokens to go with the meals, but he was not essentially a romantic man. This, however, felt romantic and she looked the part. Eyes wide, mouth parted, hands clutching at the transparent nightgown.

'You do,' he said solemnly. 'What are you afraid of? Haven't we both established that we…want the same thing?' He reached out with one hand and trailed his finger along her jaw line, then down to where her fingers were closed tightly around the shimmering, light material. 'You needn't worry. I'll be gentle.' Just talking about it was sending his normally cool, controlled nervous system through the roof.

'You don't understand…'

'You're not a virgin, are you?'

'Of course not,' Rose said indignantly, although she was guiltily aware that she really only managed to sneak into the experienced category by the skin of her teeth.

'Care to tell me about them?'

'No.'

Nick laughed. 'No need to look so shocked, Rose.'

'I suppose you do…this sort of thing all the time, don't you?'

'Sleep with women? I'm a red blooded male, Rose.'

'No, I mean… Look, what I'm trying to say is that I'm not very daring in bed, Nick.' Rose cleared her throat and looked at him defiantly. 'You can go ahead and laugh now, but that's the way it is. I haven't spent a lifetime hopping in and out of beds with men.'

'I like that,' Nick murmured. Surprisingly, he really did, although he couldn't say that he had encountered the situation before. Some of the women he had slept with were bolder than he was.

'Furthermore…'

'Furthermore?' He couldn't help himself. He leant towards her and planted a kiss on the side of her neck and he felt her shiver against him.

'I…you're not…' She wished he wouldn't look at her like that, giving her his undivided attention. 'You're…not the sort of guy…I mean, Lily normally…well, girls like Lily…'

'I'm flattered that you have such a high opinion of me.'

'I'm just talking about the way you look.'

'That's better. A bit of Rose rage.' He grinned and she smiled sheepishly back at him. 'You're beautiful, Rose.'

'Oh, please. There's no need for that, Nick.'

'Stop running yourself down,' Nick said forcefully. He gently took her fingers in his hand and unpeeled them from their stranglehold on her nightgown. Then he pushed her back onto the bed, where she fell, breathing thickly, her hair splayed out in unruly curls around her face.

What had he ever seen in those stick insects with their angular bodies and bony limbs?

He slowly pulled her nightgown over her head and there she was, in all her fulsome, voluptuous, sensual splendour. For a few seconds, Nick feasted his eyes on her and Rose looked back at him from under her lashes. Watching me, watching you, she thought, getting so turned on that she thought she might explode at any minute.

All doubts that he might have found her less attractive than the models he cavorted with were driven out of her head by the naked appreciation in his eyes.

And that did something to her. Like a dam being unblocked, every inhibition she had ever nursed about the shape of her body flowed away in a rush of wild, abandoned passion.

Nick, watching, sensed the change of mood, something in the sinuous way she moved under his raking eyes, and with a low groan he bent his head so that he could nuzzle her generous breasts.

These weren't small tomatoes, they were heavy, ripe fruit with big, defined nipples that hardened as he lavished his attention on them, suckling and feeling her wriggle underneath him in instant response.

Her skin was as smooth as satin and felt just as he had anticipated it would. Soft and womanly.

He dragged himself reluctantly away from her glorious breasts so that he could kiss her, long, slow kisses, punctuated by her soft moans.

'Touch me again,' she whispered.

'Where?'

'Where you were before…' Never had it felt so good to have her breasts touched. Having spent a life time being self-conscious about the size of them, she felt wildly liberated at Nick's obvious delight.

'Enjoyed that, did you?' he murmured, licking the side of her neck. 'My mouth all over your breasts…your spectacular breasts… I've never seen such succulent, big nipples before.'

Rose was shocked by the sexuality of his language and turned on at the same time. His voice was dark and velvety and caressing and the way he moved against her… He was as turned on as she was, of that there was no doubt.

She reached down to touch him, but he covered her hand with his.

'Not yet, my darling. I have to take things at my pace or else I might end up letting us both down.'

'I don't understand.'

'I'm so turned on for you, I have to take things slowly.'

Rose smiled, understanding, and was filled with a sense of heady power that she could have this effect on this man.

She sighed as he massaged her breasts, lifting them to his mouth so that he could continue lathering them with his tongue, taking the nipples into his mouth and teasing the throbbing buds with his teeth. Wantonly, she arched up, thrusting herself towards him and moaning loudly as he ravaged her sensitive breasts.

She curled her fingers into his hair and half opened her eyes, following his progress down and then, as he parted her moistened labia, she fell back feverishly, hardly able to believe that she was allowing such an intimate exploration of her body.

She barely knew what to expect. Her knowledge of foreplay was limited and so her body was shameless and involuntary in its arousal.

As he flicked his tongue along the delicate pink flesh, and then deeper, sliding and rubbing her most feminine area, Rose felt herself spiralling into orbit. She writhed against his exquisite invasion and knew that she lacked the will-power and fierce control not to be tipped over the edge.

With a little tug, she pulled Nick up and he laughed softly, but obediently stopped his relentless assault that threatened to send her spinning out of control.

'That was…' Rose heard her own voice and barely recognised it. It was husky and breathless.

'Mind-blowing?'

Before she could find a suitable answer, he parted her legs with his muscular thigh. 'Now let me really blow your mind,' he murmured.

It was one deep thrust. She would never have imagined that such a powerful and impressive member could enter her with such effortless ease to fill her up. He began moving inside her, slow, hard, rhythmic and he seemed to know exactly how her body worked because every time she felt herself reaching the inevitable, shattering climax, he would ease his tempo, allowing her to come back down so that he could remorselessly take her back up again.

Somewhere along the line, she was too lost in a world of sensation to really know when, he flipped them over so that she was lying on top of him, with his hands on her buttocks and her breasts dangling down, their swollen nipples perfect targets for his eager mouth.

There was no part of her body that wasn't aroused. Bliss to feel him in her even while his mouth was avidly on her.

Bliss, even, afterwards, as she eased herself off him, wonderfully fulfilled, like the cat with a very full bowl of cream.

Yes, of course, the reality of the situation was only a thought away, but she was being mad, wasn't she? Taking chances for the first time in her life? And it felt good.

'We should get some sleep now,' Rose said regretfully, 'or else we'll be like zombies in the morning.' This was like a dream, lying here, curled into him and everything making sense because she loved him, against her will. Piercing through the dream, however, was the sure and certain knowledge that there was no way she could let him know that. Unrequited love was only bearable if it remained a secret.

But…

Rose hugged this thought to herself…what if he fell in love with her? Against all odds?

Sure, she wasn't his type of woman, at least not in the expected sense, but he was seriously attracted to her, wasn't he? And he did like her, didn't he? Put those two things together and there it was, like a root beginning to take hold in the soil, the notion that in the days remaining to them she might just discover that her love stood a chance after all.

Having fought for a life that contained no nasty shocks and

hence no surprises at all, Rose now found herself walking the perilous but exhilarating path of toying with what had seemed an impossible dream.

'I'm lying in bed with you and you talk to me about getting some sleep?' Nick ran his hand along her thigh. Sleep was the last thing on his mind, never mind the hour.

Rose smiled and closed her eyes. He made her feel wanton, something she had never felt before, and she stretched her arms above her head, tempting him with the breasts he seemed to like so much, loving the way his eyes darkened as they swept over her.

Their love-making was long and languorous. He touched her everywhere and she, emboldened by him, touched him everywhere and revelled in exploring his body.

It was five before they finally fell asleep, wrapped in each other's arms, and Rose awakened to the sun doing its utmost to get a foothold in the room.

And an empty space next to her.

The dreams she had nurtured the night before, when everything had seemed tantalisingly within reach, began to dissipate like mist in the sun, but then she heard a slight sound and there he was, standing in her doorway, with a cup of coffee in his hand.

Rose sat up, pulling the sheet up to her neck, and drew her knees up with a smile.

'For you.' Nick strolled towards her with the cup of coffee.

'How long have you been up?'

'Oh, an hour or two.'

'You should have woken me up.' She yawned and took the cup from him, hoping a healthy injection of caffeine would revive her.

'And missed the sight of you sleeping the sleep of the innocent?'

Rose marvelled that someone could look so good in a pair of baggy shorts and a fairly disreputable tee shirt.

'I don't feel innocent this morning,' she confessed, shifting to make room so that he could sit on the bed next to her. 'In fact, I feel…'

'Wicked? Decadent?' He tugged the sheet down and nodded. 'Much better. I like the view far more without the sheet covering it.'

Rose blushed and grinned and gulped down some tea. *Mrs Rose Papaeliou.* Nice ring to it, she thought.

'Something like that. I've never…just had a one-night stand. Believe it or not, I'm not that kind of girl.'

'I believe you, and whoever said that this was going to be a one-night stand?'

Hope flared but she managed to keep her expression neutral. 'Give me fifteen minutes and I'll be up,' she said, changing the subject. 'What do we have planned for today?'

'Oh, I thought we would spend the rest of our time here doing a little exploring of our own.' He stood up and shot her a wolfish grin that made her toes curl in anticipation. 'How do you feel about scuba-diving?'

Rose thought that pretty much anything in the company of Nick Papaeliou would be an inviting prospect.

And there was no Lee Peng in tow. He had flown to Indonesia for a week to oversee another building project. The various people with whom they had liaised were no longer necessary, Nick informed her.

Which just left the two of them on their own and the delights of Sabah and its surroundings.

Nick thought that boredom might set in. After all, wasn't that the way of the world? And they were in each other's company twenty-four seven.

Good old common sense told him that, without those necessary absences during which batteries could be re-charged and tedium kept at bay, he was almost certain to tire of her company.

To his surprise, he didn't. She teased him mercilessly and he discovered he enjoyed it.

It was relaxing and invigorating being in her company. They scuba-dived and she proved herself pretty fearless, a side effect of having nomadic guardians, she explained, while sniggering that he seemed a little wary of the big blue sea.

They went to the local open market, which sold fruit and vegetables of every shape, size and description, many of them unrecognisable. They ate miniature figs that were sweet as sugar and drank ice-cold coconut water straight from the split coconuts that were sold in the stalls.

They dared each other to cross a bedraggled suspension bridge and then congratulated themselves afterwards by making love in a secluded part of the dense foliage and bush that fanned the river.

Without the rigid dimensions imposed by everyday life, it was easy to take that step out of sync, to explore each other without guilt and, as Rose admitted to herself, to make no attempts at holding back her headlong fall into love.

But it didn't matter because she was seeing a new side to Nick. He laughed a lot and was utterly relaxed. He had even stopped working. He took only essential calls on his mobile. Most of the time, he would glance at the number and ignore it.

Rose took that as a very good sign indeed. He wanted to spend time in her company, he enjoyed being with her to such an extent that he was willing to forgo work, and that said a great deal because, having worked alongside him, she knew that work was something Nick never, ever sidelined.

And the sex... The sex was remarkable. He was forceful considerate, inventive and utterly irresistible.

When he looked at her, she felt the hairs on the back of her neck stand on end and one touch was enough to reduce her to instant meltdown.

After a life of carefully made choices, Rose was not equipped to defend herself against the overwhelming force of what she felt.

Anyway, she didn't want to. She wanted to be reckless.

She wanted to have his arms around her as they sat on the beach and watched the sun set. She wanted him to close that bedroom door and move towards her, every muscle in his body alert with the same hunger she felt for him. She wanted to cling to her dreams that her perfect love would be returned.

Which, on the last night of their stay, brought her to the very delicate matter of how, exactly, she might find out what his intentions towards her were.

'Tonight's meal was fantastic,' she said, which was the most roundabout route she could think to discuss the fact that their holiday was now at an end. 'In fact, the food over here has been exquisite. Such flavours. I love the multi-ethnic cuisine.' Thinking that she was beginning to sound a little like a restaurant critic, she bit back the temptation to carry the theme through.

'You're gabbling, Rose. Lie back and enjoy the stars and the sound of the sea.'

Rose obediently lay down next to him on the wide beach towel provided courtesy of the hotel, which seemed to know that sun loungers were not to everyone's taste. Especially, she thought, late at night when you wanted to be physically close to someone. Like now.

She tried to submerge herself in the ambience but her thoughts were whirring around in her head and she finally said, casually, 'Bit of a change, all this, isn't it? From London, I mean…'

'Huge change.'

'Be strange to go back tomorrow.'

'Very strange.' He sounded faintly surprised at that admission. 'But reality's never further than a stone's throw away.'

'I thought that was rats.'

'In my line of work, the two are often interlinked.'

Rose could feel him grinning in the dark but she didn't want to relax and enjoy his sense of humour, as she had done for the past few days. She wanted to pry beneath the surface and find out what happened next in their chapter, because she was sure that there would be a next.

'Will you miss…being here?' With me?

'All good things come to an end.' Nick shrugged, his hand, under her neck, hanging, almost touching her breast. 'That's just the way it is.'

'Which…' Rose decided to take the bull by the horns because they could sit around talking in metaphors all night and get nowhere '…leaves *us* where?'

Well, Nick thought with disappointment, it had to happen eventually. The bubble had to burst. He had idiotically thought that Rose, who was in a league of her own, would be the exception to the rule, the one woman who didn't start questioning the future and trying, thereby, to pin him down to promises of ever afters he had no intention of making.

'Well, I think we can safely say that your stint working for me is now over. Shy of a week or so, but we've accomplished what we set out to do, wouldn't you agree? You must be looking forward to getting back to your old routine. Are you?'

'Yes, of course I am.' In truth, she had barely missed her old job and was certainly not looking forward to returning to the grindstone having sampled the excitement of working for Nick, where every day brought new challenges. However, she wasn't a fool. She might have abandoned common sense, she might have dared to hope that her flight of fancy would bring her the result she wanted, but she could read nuances as well as the next person. Better. Over the years her ingrained sensitivity had fine-tuned her antennae and her antennae were now telling her that he was backing away from giving her a direct answer for a reason and there could only be one reason. Whatever he felt for her, it wasn't love. It wasn't even enough to give her any kind of commitment. The man who had always walked away from relationships of any depth was walking away now and Rose felt as though her lifeblood were draining out of her system.

What had she been thinking? That the way his eyes darkened when he saw her naked counted as love? Or that the easy way they talked and laughed and touched really meant something?

Inside she was hurting so much that she suddenly couldn't bear the feel of his arm around her. Outside, though, she controlled her voice and schooled her expression even though he couldn't see her face and made sure to sound as calm as she could as she started to chat about what had been happening in her old job, updates from her friends whom she had barely seen over the past few months.

'Naturally, this doesn't have to mean the end of…what we have,' Nick murmured, and Rose could feel him turn towards her. What, she wanted to ask, exactly do we have? For him, yet another pointless relationship based on satisfying sex and for her…more heartbreak, more involvement, more misery in the end.

'Oh, I think it should, really…'

'You don't mean that.' Nick turned completely towards

her and tilted her head so that he could kiss the side of her neck and Rose shrugged him off and sat up.

'I do.' She looked over her shoulder at him. Moonlight becomes him...wasn't there a song that went like that? He was just wearing an old tee shirt and a pair of faded jeans, but she knew every inch of his perfect body now, knew the lazy strength and muscular body encased in the casual clothing. She wondered how she could ever have thought that he might actually fall in love with her, the way she had fallen in love with him.

Would he return to England and be embarrassed to be seen with her? He had told her often enough that he loved her curves, found them incredibly sexy, that stick-thin, in comparison, was a turn-off. But that was here, where everything had been in a state of unreal suspension. She would bet her newly refurbished house that the minute they stepped back onto English soil stick-thin would suddenly be desirable because stick-thin represented the sort of model type he needed hanging on his arm.

He would always run true to form and she had been a fool to have thought otherwise. He was, and always had been, out of her league.

Rose stood up and dusted herself down. He, of course, was still lying on the towel, hands behind his head, probably, she thought, convinced that he could talk her round. Maybe for a few more romps in the hay back in England, where he would keep her hidden away and out of sight.

'This has been great.' She gesticulated vaguely around her. 'The scenery, the atmosphere, the romance of being out of England and in the hot sun. Now it's finishing...'

'You asked what was going to become of us.' Nick sat up. 'That implies that you consider us an item.'

'I meant in connection with work,' she lied. 'I thought it

would be awkward being stuck in each other's company, pretending that nothing had happened between us.'

'Stuck in each other's company?'

'I'm sorry. I didn't mean it that way. What I meant was…' Now he was standing up, which instantly made her feel a lot less assured. 'Look, this has been brilliant. I never thought…well, my first impressions of you weren't all that flattering but I've enjoyed every minute of being here with you. We had fun, didn't we?'

Nick couldn't quite believe his ears. Shouldn't he be the one giving the Dear John lecture? Shouldn't he be the one doing the letting down slowly and gently?

Anyway, whoever said that it had to end just yet? Sure, he didn't want a strings-attached relationship. Never had, probably never would. Which didn't mean that they couldn't continue enjoying each other until time did its thing and they both decided to move on.

'Sure, it's been fun.' He hooked his thumbs in the pockets of his jeans and stared at her. That sexy body…that light, infectious laughter… Well, this was her choice and the right one, really. 'And I'm glad you're…so calm about this…'

'What did you expect?' Rose asked lightly. 'Tears and histrionics?'

Nick shrugged and began walking back to their rooms. This was most definitely not how he had expected to spend his last night in Borneo. 'Maybe nothing so extreme,' he grated as she fell in step with him. 'You're not the tears and histrionics kind of girl, are you?'

Certainly not in public and definitely not when she'd made a complete idiot of herself.

'Not really.'

'And I'm glad about that.' He stopped and Rose continued

walking for a few steps before turning around to look at him. 'I wouldn't want to have hurt you in any way. You know me, Rose.' He laughed softly although something inside him felt slightly sick. Probably, he figured, because he had had the rug pulled very neatly from under his feet. Well, everyone needed a shake-up now and again and he was no exception. It hurt because the feeling was so damned alien to him. 'I can't give promises of commitment and settling down.'

'And I wouldn't want them,' she said quickly. 'Certainly not from you. We clicked in bed, but there's so much more to relationships than just clicking in the sack.'

Nick wasn't sure he much liked that, but he gave her a brief nod, which could have been agreement or simply acknowledgement of what she was trying to say.

'But, and I never thought that I would say this, I'm grateful to you, and not just because you bailed me out of a financial mess. I'm looking forward to going back to my old job, but you've given me the confidence to think about new pastures, not to rely on just doing the same thing day in and day out and thinking that it's fine because I know the routine.'

'Glad to be of service,' Nick told her coolly.

'Course, I'll make sure that I have all the written reports ready for you by next Monday.'

'No need.'

'What do you mean?'

'I'm no longer convinced that I'll be siting Borneo for my hotel.'

'Why not?' Rose asked, astounded at his U-turn. 'It's an amazing island. And you've put in so much time in getting to know it.'

'Yes, it's an amazing island and if tourism is to kick in, then I would rather not be the one to introduce it. It's easy for a unique place like this to lose its innocence because of rampant commercialism.' And besides, he thought angrily, Borneo would forever remind him of her. They had spent some pretty intense days together and she had imprinted too much of it with her stamp. How could he ever walk along this stretch of beach again without thinking about her? And that wouldn't do. He had let his guard down, allowed her to get under his skin, and let this, he thought, be a lesson to him.

She was delivering some heartfelt speech about tasteful and controlled tourism and the benefits to a local community and he sliced through her ramblings with dismissive ease, pleased to have her reduced to silence.

'You make some valid points, but my decision is made.' Churlish would be to make a big deal of the fact that she had, like it or not, ended their relationship. Churlish, in other words, would be to allow his ego to be involved. On the other hand, he could be as relieved as she appeared to be that the whole thing was over and, honestly, he was. Good while it lasted but all good things came to an end and it was best to part company on good terms. The ideal scenario when it came to the opposite sex, if he thought about it.

'So…' he injected some warmth into his voice as they began to stroll back to the hotel complex '…all packed?'

'Check.'

'Including those ridiculous souvenirs you insisted on buying at the market a couple of days ago?'

'They weren't ridiculous. You'll be sorry you didn't invest in a couple yourself when you get back to England and realise that they would have looked very fetching on your walls.' She kept her voice as light as she could, but now the bantering that had led her to think of what they had as something special hurt beyond endurance.

'Name two places where colourful masks would have blended in.'

'You mean against the stark white walls and expensive abstracts?'

Rose heard herself conducting this perfectly normal conversation from a distance, almost as though she were hovering over herself, watchful and detached.

When they were finally standing outside their rooms, she smiled at him, gratefully, she hoped, and stuck out her hand, which he pointedly ignored.

'That's a bit ridiculous,' he drawled. 'Yes, we've both reached the same conclusion that this was a holiday fling best left on the island, but I think shaking hands is slightly ludicrous.' He bent and kissed her on the mouth, but this was a fond, farewell kiss, devoid of the urgency and hunger she had become accustomed to, and it hurt like hell.

It did, however, set the tone for the next day, during which they were affable, polite and very, very busy. Flights, work that Nick suddenly remembered needed to be done and books that Rose decided should have been read.

She could already feel the mantle of England settling back over her long before the plane finally touched down at Heathrow.

She had feverishly wondered how they would actually part company when the moment arrived, but in all events it was an anticlimax. Nick spotted someone he knew and, before she could brace herself for the hellishness of the final goodbye, he was kissing her fondly on the cheek and excusing himself. Would she be okay to handle a taxi back herself? Just a couple of things he wanted to talk to Ed Duggins about…take care of yourself…hope the house lives up to expectations… The usual platitudes, but his mind was already somewhere else. He had moved on.

Rose went directly to her house. She had been there almost every day to supervise the work in progress and had left her painter and decorator in charge of replastering and wallpapering over the mess made by the builders.

At any rate, that was exciting. She was delivered to her door in a black cab and, once inside the house, wandered around taking in the changes, and there were a fair few of those. Terry had done an excellent job. Everywhere looked new and smelt new.

And it was all paid for. She told herself that she should be over the moon, but as it turned out the only thing she had to smile about was her phone call to her sister.

Lily was coming home. Just for a couple of weeks because the leading man had apparently done something unfortunate to his ankle. Filming would skirt around him, but her scenes were already shot.

Her voice down the other end of the phone was like a tonic and Rose couldn't help herself. For once she wasn't the one holding everything together. And for once Lily was the strong half, soothing, reassuring, safe in her own area of expertise—namely men.

'Don't worry, Rosie. I'm coming home and everything's gonna be fine. Wait and see.'

Somewhere in middle America, Lily smiled to herself as she hung up the phone—Rose needed her and that felt good, and, even better, she was going to make sure that everything really was all right for her sister.

CHAPTER EIGHT

'Now that you've been back nearly two weeks, I think it's time we went out and had a good time. I'm heading back to America next Wednesday and I can't bear the thought of leaving you alone here when you're so miserable.'

Rose looked at her sister and tried to imagine whether she was capable of ever having a good time again. Not a word from Nick since they had returned to England. Not a phone call, not a message left on the answering machine, nothing. It was as though she had never existed in his eyes.

For Lily's sake, she had played down her feelings, but her talents as an actor must have been less successful than she had thought because here was her sister now, looking at her worriedly, in fact the way she had looked at Lily many a time in the past. The shoe was very securely on the other foot.

'I'm not miserable, Lily. I'm tired. And, besides, I haven't got time to have a good time.' Rose looked at her sister over the rim of her mug.

'That doesn't make sense.'

'Sure it does. I mean, I've only been back at my old job a few days and you wouldn't believe the stack of work that was waiting for me. A lovely little collection of jobs no one else wanted to do.' Every single one of which was utterly boring,

she was tempted to add, but didn't because she was determined, after her initial confession and shameful blubbing down
the phone, not to make a fuss. She had lost her head and had
her moment of madness and now was time to pick up the pieces
and not wallow in a tide of self-pity. At least, not in public.

'But it's a Saturday, Rose.' Lily sighed dramatically.

'Don't worry about me, I want you to go out and have fun.
As you said, Lily, you'll be heading back in a few days. You
want to catch up with all your fans before you go.' Rose
smiled at her sister. The phone had not stopped ringing since
Lily had arrived back. Friends wanting to meet up and, according to Lily, who had developed a healthy streak of
cynicism since working in America, not-nearly-friends who
wanted to rub shoulders with someone in the movie business.

'No. You and I are going to go out tonight. Nice little jazz
club in the West End. You can get your glad rags on and I'll
ask a couple of people I met when I was in America who are
over here as well. We'll make it a cosy evening.' Lily was not
about to take no for an answer. She had promised herself that
she would make sure that Rose was just fine by the time she
returned to America and she wasn't about to jettison that goal.
She gave her a coaxing but implacable smile.

Several hours later and Rose wasn't sure whether to be
amused or alarmed by her sister's newly acquired ability to
chivvy.

Chivvied from shop to shop because retail therapy was, apparently, the best form of therapy. Then from shop to beauty
parlour where Rose's short nails were turned into works of
art with pearly pink nail polish. Then onward from the beauty
parlour to the hairdresser's, conveniently and suspiciously
pre-booked, where her naturally curly hair underwent some
weird metamorphosis and emerged a fabulous tumble of

windblown curls rather than her usual unkempt, unmanageable mess. And brilliantly gold, thanks to some clever mixing of dyes. Lots of highlights everywhere.

Lily pronounced herself satisfied and they returned to the house energised with several carrier bags and, in Rose's case, a complete makeover.

Course, she thought, she would never be lean and glamorous like her sister, but she hadn't exactly looked fat in the dressing rooms.

'You've lost weight,' Lily announced airily, not for the first time reading her sister's mind as she dumped the bags on the kitchen table. She poured Rose a glass of wine to get her in the mood, and plonked herself down on one of the chairs. 'I kinda liked the old you,' Lily said wistfully. 'Cuddly and comfortable.'

Rose wondered whether that was how Nick had seen her. As cuddly and comfortable, like an old cushion that was just right for sleeping with when nothing better was available. She rescued herself from pointlessly worrying the thought and smiled as Lily went on to talk about the people she had met in America, and their obsession with food. They either seemed to eat too much or eat too little. Doughnut emporiums squatted alongside organic health food shops and she had seen people leaving their gyms, still perspiring from their workouts, to head directly to the nearest hot-dog stand where they would proceed to order the largest of everything.

Rose was quietly convinced that Lily would return to England. She had confided on more than one occasion, looking over her shoulder as though one of those Bigwigs she kept mentioning might pop out from behind a bush, that there was too much pressure in America to be thin, to be competitive, to suck up to the right people. Lily, having inherited

Tony and Flora's basic bohemian disregard for personal wealth, couldn't understand why everyone seemed so willing to jump through hoops for yet more money, which they obviously didn't need.

'Anyway, you're sick of me going on about this.' She grinned. 'Maybe I'll just return to London when I'm done there. My CV will be a whole lot healthier, thanks to Nick, and I can just get a nice little job in a soap opera.'

Nick. Not once had she asked her sister whether she had seen Nick. She had told herself that she wasn't interested, that the past was the past, but she knew, really, that she was just scared. Scared that she might want her sister to tell her too much. Scared that the floodgates, which she was trying hard to close, would crash open again and she would be lost.

'Right.' All assertive once again, Lily stood up, topped Rose's glass of wine with a fraction more, and ordered her to go and get changed but to do absolutely nothing with her make-up because she, Lily, would do it for her.

'You wouldn't believe the tips I've got from the girls who make me up.' She laughed. 'Believe me, it's all in the brush strokes.'

'You're chivvying again.' But Rose laughed because it was just so good not to be on her own. She had missed Lily, but only now was she realising by how much.

'And it feels good. Now I can understand why you spent your life chivvying me around as a kid.'

There was no rush and Rose took her time getting dressed. Yes, she really had lost weight and it suited her. She had also been coerced into buying a little black number that she would never have dared to have worn a few months ago. It had a plunging neckline, one of her great no-noes previously, and exposed more than a generous eyeful of cleavage. With high heels, she felt quite pleased with herself. The dress fitted snugly to the waist, then flared out to just above the knees.

By the time Lily had sorted out her costume jewellery and applied the make-up, Rose felt her spirits lift. She could almost believe her own mantra that she was well rid of Nick, that life was just about to begin, that all experience, in hindsight, was good experience, that he was little more than a dot on her learning curve brought on by temporary insanity. Of course, the two and a half glasses of white wine helped.

They took a taxi and just when Rose was beginning to warm to the idea of not staying in, Lily dropped the bombshell.

Nick was going to be there. Well, he might be there. But don't worry about it. Wouldn't it be good to prove to him how much she had managed to get her act together? There was no need to fuss. She looked fabulous. She couldn't spend her days scuttling away from the possibility of seeing him again. Sooner or later the time would come when she would meet him because she, Lily, remained good friends with him and grateful for everything he had done to help her with her career. Never run scared, that was the key thing.

Rose, despairingly, toyed with the idea of demanding that the taxi driver turn around and take her back home.

Then, if not back home, at least to the nearest pub so that she could fortify her nerves with a couple more glasses of wine.

But she was given little opportunity to object because Lily, with all her newly acquired bossiness, kept up a never-ending monologue for most of the trip, and Rose glumly took on board that her sister had a point. Why should she be scared? It wasn't as if Nick had guessed her shameful secret. He had no idea that what to him had been a fling had, for her, been the love of a lifetime. She looked good and if there was one thing he had done for her, it had been to inject a level of confidence in her appearance that she had never really had. He had made her feel sexy and the residue of that confidence was still there. The little black dress looked great and if he did turn up, big if because, as Lily had pointed out, he was mega busy and the invite had been last-minute, then she would damn well show him that she was doing fine.

The jazz club was tucked away in a side road a million miles away on the other side of London. Rose had no idea how her sister had managed to discover the place, but it was certainly popular. Despite being early, the venue was already beginning to fill up. She had no time to wonder whether she was feeling nervous about meeting Nick because over the next hour or so she was wrapped up in the business of meeting Lily's friends, a fair few of whom were American and flatteringly thrilled to be in a genuine British club and not one of those that catered for the loaded tourists.

This was new for Rose, this feeling of blending in with a crowd of people, all strangers to her. She was determined not to drink too much, but the music was sexy and, although she stuck to wine, she found her glass being replaced without her having to ask or even make her way to the bar.

The dress, she thought, was proving even more effective than she could ever have dared to hope.

Several men seemed to find her fascinating, although it was hard to tell because the atmospheric lighting bordered on downright dark. Certainly one in particular had taken her under his wing and had been responsible for at least two glasses of wine, the last of which Rose was now drinking very slowly indeed as she listened to him tell her about his latest film, a short *film noir*, which had had a very successful première at the Cannes festival.

Lily had asked a lot of her old friends, but most of the new faces belonged to the world of film and media. Rose had never met so many men who seemed to be film producers. They were very entertaining, even if she had never heard of a single one of the films they had produced. A lot of them, she noticed, sported pony-tails, which looked very trendy. Miles apart, she thought nastily, from Nick, who was as traditional as they went when it came to fashion. Long hair and jewellery on men, he had told her, were strictly for hippies, and she had laughed and accused him of being narrow-minded.

The memory made her heart constrict.

At least he wasn't around. She had kept one beady eye open so that she could take appropriate measures to avoid him, but it was now after ten and he was nowhere in sight, obviously too busy to get away.

Disappointment bit into her and she favoured her companion with a wide, reckless smile.

Which was when she spotted him, standing on the other side of the room, with a leggy red-haired woman on his arm. She looked as though she had been poured into her small silver dress.

Rose felt her heart skip a beat and, weirdly, the noise, the people, even the band playing a slow number on the little raised podium, seemed to fade away, leaving just the sight of him, as sexy as she remembered, in a pair of dark-coloured trousers and a white shirt, casually rolled to the elbows.

Well, he seemed to have managed to relegate her to the history books in no time at all, Rose thought bitterly. Less than a month and he was back to his cover-girl babes.

She gulped down what was left in her glass and concentrated on what the man by her side was saying. His name was Ted, although his friends, for reasons that escaped her, called him Splice, and he was giving her the low-down on the people he had met at the Cannes Festival, a warts-and-all account that would have been hilarious had her attention not been suddenly hijacked by her ex-lover, now excusing himself and heading for the bar while the red-haired beauty sashayed over to the nearest group of men, one of whom she clearly knew. The world of actors, models and musicians was a very small one, Lily had told her.

Rose gaily accepted another drink from Ted Splice, as she called him in her head, and was making sure not to look in the direction of the redhead just in case Nick returned to his date and noticed her staring, when she felt the tap on her shoulder.

She spun round and there he was. She'd been certain she hadn't been noticed, but he must have seen her as he was making his way back from the bar.

Rose felt her heart skip a beat, then she produced the same sparkly smile she had perfected with Ted.

'Good heavens.. Fancy seeing you here. How are you?' She noticed that he failed to produce a reciprocal smile. In fact, his expression was cool and Rose was suddenly enraged that he should chuck her aside and then, as if that weren't bad enough, treat her to the cold shoulder.

'You seem to be having a good time,' Nick drawled, giving her a leisurely appraisal.

'Oh, I am.'

'Bit of a change for you, isn't it? This kind of thing?'

'Well, you know what they say about a change being as good as a rest. I hadn't expected it to be quite as large as this, but I'm having a brilliant time, meeting loads of really interesting people.'

'So I couldn't help but notice.'

His voice dripped ice and Rose wondered whether, having an ego the size of a house, he had expected her to be sitting indoors pining for him. Little could he guess that she had pretty much been doing just that until tonight.

'What about you?' she asked politely. 'Having a good time? Did you come with anyone? I guess you know quite a few of the people here anyway…' She was gratified to notice that even the subdued lighting couldn't quite hide his dark flush and she gave him her most innocent look.

'As a matter of fact, I did come with someone. She's over there somewhere.' He indicated somewhere behind her while keeping his eyes firmly fixed on her face, and Rose dutifully turned around to see the redhead looking daggers at her.

'Oh, dear. Your date doesn't look awfully happy that you've abandoned her. You'd better run along before she blows a fuse.'

Nick, whose mood seemed to be deteriorating by the second, scowled. 'My date is more than capable of taking care of herself for a few minutes.' He bared his teeth in a smile. 'Besides, I don't think she would begrudge me catching up with an old…friend…' Of course he had known that she would be there and he had brought along the arm candy to remind himself that he had done the right thing, they had both done the right thing—parted company because at the end of the day she was a settling-down kind of girl and he was a no-commitment kind of guy. That was just the way it was. He liked variety. The redhead filled that role.

'I don't think there's much to catch up on.' Rose frowned and made a show of giving his remark all the attention it deserved. 'I'm back at my old job and enjoying it and…' she could be as cool and dismissive as he was '…you were very useful in teaching me that madness isn't always a bad thing. As you can see, I've taken that advice to heart.' She laughed gaily. 'I'd have steered a million miles away from something like this in the past—as you pointed out…'

He had been useful? Nick didn't appreciate the compliment, not at all.

'There's madness and there's stupidity, Rose,' he gritted. 'Madness is breaking out of your comfort zone and coming here tonight…'

'And stupidity?' She was pretty sure she wasn't going to like his answer, but that, in a way, would surely work for her, because how on earth would she ever get closure if she carried on loving him? Let him show himself in all his arrogant glory, she willed.

'Stupidity is wearing that dress.'

Rose's mouth fell open in shock. She gave an incredulous laugh. 'You object to *my* dress?' She glanced significantly over her shoulder to where his date gave the term skimpy clothing a whole new meaning.

'That's completely different,' Nick growled.

'Oh, and why is that? Because she's tall and skinny and can carry off wearing handkerchiefs better than me?'

'Because…' Because she's as sexy as a runner bean, Nick thought savagely. He deeply resented the fact that the woman standing in front of him, flaunting herself to all and sundry, was still on his mind, despite all his efforts to wipe her out. 'Because,' he grated, 'you could land yourself in a situation you wouldn't be able to handle dressed like that. Did you look in the mirror before you left your house? Do you have any idea how much of your…you is on show?'

'It's been nice chatting to you, Nick. Now, I think I see Splice coming with my drink.'

'Splice?'

'That's his nickname.' Rose smiled sweetly and walked away without giving him the chance to continue the conversation. Out of the corner of her eye, she saw her sister looking in her direction and she waved cheerfully, not wanting to spoil the evening by having Lily worrying about her. Again.

The minute Lily could escape, however, Rose was dismayed to find that she was by her side and Rose just knew what her sister was going to say.

'What on earth was going on with the two of you back then?' Lily asked, jumping straight in with both feet and making Rose feel even guiltier that her sister had noticed more than she had first suspected. 'What was Nick saying to you?'

'Lily, never you mind that. I'm not going to spoil your last Saturday night in London by repeating what that man had the nerve to say.' At one in the morning, the crowd was beginning to thin out. Most of Lily's friends had headed off, with a couple of the guys insisting on giving Rose their phone numbers although she, tactfully, declined to return the favour. Still, it was flattering even if she couldn't get Nick's nasty remark about her dress out of her head.

He, as luck would have it, was still around somewhere, with the redhead clutching him possessively as if scared that he might disappear unless physically restrained. Which, of course, he would. Rose, consistently aware of his presence, made sure to live up to her statement that she was having a brilliant time. She was pretty sure that, at one point, Ted had even asked if she would consider starring in one of his productions, which had resulted in fits of laughter on her part. She had half hoped that Nick might have glanced over at that point and witnessed for himself just how much fun she was having.

Wrapped up in her mental reverie, she became aware of Lily pressing her for details, and eventually she gave in, telling her that he had criticised her dress and dared to suggest that she was somehow sending off the wrong messages and then, having done that, would be incapable of taking care of herself.

Lily was nodding, taking it all in, and finally said, 'You can't let him get away with that.'

'What do you mean?'

'You should be angry. Fuming!'

'Well…yes…I am…'

'You need to march over there and let him know that you're not just anyone. In fact, you need to let him know that you're more than capable of taking care of yourself. In fact, Splice was mightily impressed by you…' Lily glanced at her nails, painted a vibrant, deep purple. 'Nick might just want to know that he's not the only guy interested in you…'

'He isn't interested in me.'

'I'll distract Cat—'

'Cat?' What cat? What was Lily on about?

'His date for the evening. She likes to call herself that. Her real name's Nancy. I met her briefly in my modelling days.'

'I don't think—'

'Quite right. Don't think. Thinking just complicates matters.' She pushed Rose out towards where Nick was standing and holding court with several of the pony-tailed men.

There she went. Chivvying again. What was she supposed to say to Nick? She just wanted to go home, but the redhead was being suitably distracted and the pony-tail brigade was breaking up, heading off, leaving her alone with him.

'My sister wanted your girlfriend to meet a friend of hers…' was all Rose could think of saying. 'Her name's Cat, I gather.'

'She's not my girlfriend.'

'Oh. Date, in that case.' Rose shrugged as if she was bored with the business of him splitting hairs. 'It's been nice meeting you again, Nick. I'm off now.'

'Wait just a minute.' He caught hold of her arm as she

was turning away and Rose tensed. 'How much have you had to drink?'

'What I've had to drink has nothing to do with you.'

'No? How are you going to get back to your house?'

'In a taxi. With Lily.' Where was her sister, anyway? 'Or not, as the case may be.' Her skin burnt where he was holding her, bringing back memories she wanted to forget, and she looked at him with unhidden hostility.

'I'll take you home.'

'You'll do no such thing.' Alarm and panic slammed into her with such force that she took a step backwards.

'Your sister's not around and nor are any of those creeps who were drooling down your front all night.'

'They were not creeps. In fact—' she smirked '—Ted's desperate to get in touch with me. He's a movie producer, you know.' Or maybe it was advertising. She couldn't quite remember.

That clarified something in Nick's head. The woman might think that she was embarking on some crazy hedonistic life-style, but she had no idea what she was letting herself in for. He had met sufficient movie producers in his time, thanks to his history of dating women in the modelling or acting business, and he knew that kindly, thoughtful and caring were not adjectives commonly used to describe them.

'Did you bring a jacket?'

'You are *not* taking me home.' Rose looked around desperately for her sister. 'Anyway, you can't bring a date and then abandon her. How is your girlfriend going to get home?'

'Wait right here.'

Rose had no intention of doing any such thing. She tripped along behind Nick and reached her sister just as he was explaining the need to deliver Rose back to the house unless Lily was on her way out. Which she wasn't, never mind the pointed looks and contorted gestures Rose was delivering behind Nick's back.

'I've got to stay until the last person leaves,' Lily said gaily, ignoring her sister. 'Only polite. And Cat can't possibly go yet. Not when I've just introduced her to Joe Carr here. Can you, Cat?'

Rose had never seen anyone truly wriggle on the horns of a dilemma, but Cat did now. She was obviously furious at the thought of her date clearing off with another woman, even though the woman was no competition, but the prospect of networking with someone from the film industry who might prove useful later down the line was irresistible.

She did the best she could under the circumstances and all credit to her, Rose thought nastily, she did it well.

'Call me,' she purred to Nick, and then reached forward to pull him towards her. From behind, Rose watched the slender pale fingers with perfectly painted long red nails comb his dark hair and, from what she could see, he was thoroughly enjoying the kiss.

The sight made her feel sick to her stomach. What further proof could she have that he had forgotten her? Wearing a sexy black dress and flirting madly with people whose names she could barely remember suddenly struck her as very sad.

Lily, she noticed, was staring at her, and Rose composed her features into bland indifference, which was the stance she maintained as Nick ushered her out of the club, fetching her jacket *en route*, and into the sharp early morning air.

His driver was waiting outside and she climbed into the back seat of the car in silence.

'So…' Nick slammed the door behind him and turned to her '…you're suddenly very quiet.'

'I'm tired.'

'We still have a conversation to finish.'

'What conversation?' Rose looked at him with a sigh. 'We don't have anything left to finish, Nick. We've both moved on.'

Nick frowned at her. 'Which doesn't mean that I don't still have…' feelings for you. Except that there was something somehow significant about saying that. So he avoided it. 'A sense of responsibility towards you. After all, Rose, we were lovers, whether you like it or not.'

'And now you're scratching another notch on your bedpost. If it makes you feel better, I absolve you from all responsibility towards me. I don't need your misguided sense of duty, Nick. You employed me because you were Lily's friend and you felt sorry for me when I was in a financial mess. Now you feel sorry for me because—'

'I don't feel sorry for you,' he snapped sharply.

'Then what? I don't want you to involve yourself in my life.'

She slid her eyes over to him. Earlier, she had felt tipsy and mellow and just that little bit out of control. Right now, she couldn't have felt more sober. 'Do you always feel as though you've got to look out for the hapless women you've been involved with?'

'You consider yourself hapless?'

'I consider myself…changed…'

'So you said earlier.' Nick's voice was acid. 'I wasn't sure whether or not to be flattered by the adjective you used for me as useful.'

No, he wouldn't be. Useful wasn't exactly a sexy term. It was probably also a little too close to used for Nick's liking, but Rose didn't care because wasn't that what he did with all the women who littered his life?

'And people don't change overnight, Rose. You can't

suddenly turn into a woman who lives life on the edge. You've never been that kind of woman. You remember telling me how much Tony and Flora turned you off the idea of taking chances because of the lifestyle they chose? They wanted you to want adventure. Instead you found your adventure in books.'

'Yes, and now I've decided that they were right after all. I'm too young to bury myself in books when there's a whole world out there waiting to be lived.'

'And you intend to live every minute of it in revealing clothes.'

'So what if I do? What business is it of yours? You've rescued me once. There's no need to make a habit of it.'

The driver was at long last approaching the house and Rose located her glittery handbag and tucked her jacket a little tighter around her shoulders, ready to sprint from car to front door in the shortest possible time.

The frame of the redhead's fingers clawing into Nick's hair repeated itself endlessly in her head, like a snippet of film viewed in slow motion.

'I'm not trying to rescue you,' Nick grated, leaping out of the car as soon as it had stopped.

'Don't let me keep you.' Rose turned the key in the lock, pushed open the door and smiled sweetly at him.

The woman was crazy, Nick thought. Had she no idea what sort of temptation she presented to a red-blooded male? Wearing a dress like that with everything on display? Her cleavage was just a teasing reminder of her succulent breasts, which he considered outrageously hugged by the thin, stretchy fabric. If she was his, he thought, there was no way that he would let her out of the house looking like that.

'You're not getting rid of me that quickly,' he growled, pushing the door wide open with the flat of his hand and stepping inside the house before she could shut the door in his face.

Rose spun round and folded her arms. 'We have nothing to say to one another, Nick.'

'You're not to leave the house dressed the way you were tonight.' Where the hell had that come from?

'You're telling me what I can wear?'

'For your own good.' He flushed darkly and walked away from her incredulous expression, into the sitting room where he prowled restlessly before perching against the bay window so that he could look at her framed in the doorway.

'For my own good?'

'Stop parroting me,' Nick said irritably. He failed to see why she would stare at him as though he had taken leave of his senses when, as far as he was concerned, he was being perfectly reasonable and pretty decent.

'You may think you know what you're letting yourself in for, but you don't,' he informed her bluntly, and Rose's mouth fell open a fraction further. So it was fine for him to practically make love in front of an audience with a bimbo who seemed to have an allergy to fabric, but he still found it perfectly acceptable to lecture *her* about her dress code and her general code of behaviour.

She had never known anything so hypocritical in her life. She opened her mouth a few times to say something and instead succeeded in giving a goldfish impression.

'Not only is it dangerous for you to dress like that because you're giving off all the wrong signals, but you're dressing for the wrong crowd anyway. Half the men there were gay and the other half would put Casanova to shame when it comes to scruples.'

'And since you don't fall into the gay category, Nick, we both know which one you belong to.'

'We're not talking about me.'

'No, we're talking about double standards. Maybe I'm in search of an unscrupulous man. Have you considered that? Maybe my Big Change involves taking a break from the safe guy and just seeing what the grass is like on the other side.'

'You know you don't mean that.'

'Really?' Rose fumbled in her bag and whipped out the business card on which Ted Splice had written his various numbers. She waved it in the air as if proving her point, as if one small piece of cardboard were actually a key to the gates of wildness, adventure and scandal. As if she would ever, in a million years, seriously consider dating a man whose nickname was Splice.

'I didn't tell you this, but Ted and I are going out…on a date…next Saturday to…' She named the first restaurant that came into her head, which, unfortunately, was a cheap and cheerful pizza place not a hundred miles away from where she lived. 'And who knows what might happen once we've finished eating?'

CHAPTER NINE

THE advantage to the cheap and cheerful pizza place lay in its size. It was vast and, at eight thirty on a Saturday evening, brimming with families.

Nick hadn't intended to end up there. In fact, for the better part of the week he had told himself that he had more important things to do than to waste time on one highly infuriating woman. If, he piously concluded, she wanted to hurl herself into the party scene, then she could damn well live with the consequences, and consequences there most certainly would be. If she paraded her body with a type like movie producer Ted, then she might just as well have Available stamped across her forehead in large neon lettering.

Especially with this Ted character, about whom he had managed to source some information. The man had been in and out of rehab like a yo-yo, which was not exactly a notable event in the world he lived in, but Nick could not think of Rose seriously dating a guy like that. In fact, he had discovered that he couldn't think of her seriously dating any guy without feeling ferociously possessive.

Possessive over a woman.

The notion, when it first trickled into his head, was so unbelievable that it bordered on amusing. He had never been a possessive man, had never been jealous, had prided himself on his controlled approach to relationships.

Six days down the line, there was nothing amusing about it. He thought of the man's oily hands stripping Rose of her skimpy black dress, unhooking her bra, feasting his eyes on her big, beautiful breasts and felt sick.

He should never have allowed what they had to finish. That was the problem. Things that ended prematurely became unattainable objects of desire simply because basic need hadn't been sated. He had thought himself in control of what they had and only now realised that what they had had been controlling him.

But still. Going to the pizza place had not been an option. He had just somehow found himself driving over there well before she and her date were due to arrive, found himself taking the quietest and least noticeable table at the very far corner of the room where he was half shielded by an oversized plastic plant in drastic need of dusting. He found himself doing all this and it was almost as if his head had no say in the matter.

The pizza he ordered for himself as he waited was surprisingly good. The wine slightly less so, but nevertheless drinkable.

By eight-thirty, when neither Rose nor her date had yet arrived, he was smugly contemplating the very satisfying theory that Ted the movie producer had stood her up. He imagined her sitting bleakly in her sitting room, wondering whether or not to text, knowing that this was the first nail in the coffin of her new lifestyle.

She might even, he thought with a kick of real pleasure, be glumly admitting to herself that he, Nick, had been right after all to warn her off the man.

This was such a pleasing fantasy that he almost missed them. Feeling a little ridiculous because of his cloak-and-dagger tactics, Nick watched them through the fronds of the plastic plant, watched them taken through to a table uncomfortably sandwiched between two families with exuberant kids.

She had steered away from wearing anything revealing, but, instead of finding this acceptable, he darkly decided that she looked even sexier in her short grey skirt, her too-short grey skirt and neatly tailored blouse. She could almost have been going out to work except for the two top buttons of her shirt, which were undone. Nick was pretty sure that if he noticed that little detail, then so did Ted the reformed producer. He couldn't actually see the man's face because Ted had his back to him, but it was easy to imagine those beady little eyes flicking rapaciously over her body while he tried to work out the fastest way of getting her into bed.

Nick tensed and he finished his glass of wine and signalled the waitress over so that he could order something else. Coffee and dessert, because now he was condemned to remain where he was or risk being seen on the way out.

Not that he had plans to leave until they did. He sat back and folded his hands on his stomach and watched.

Rose, sitting on the opposite side of the room, was glumly regretting the impulse that had led her to this place.

She had reacted to Nick's horrible, patronising attitude towards her a week ago by fabricating a non-existent date with a man who had been flattering and pleasant enough for a couple of hours but several thousand light years away from someone she would ever have considered going out with.

In fact, there had been no need for her to telephone Ted at all, but she had been prompted into doing so for all the wrong reasons. Hurt at seeing Nick with another woman, anger that he should dare tell her how to live her life having done such a comprehensive job of ruining it, and a stubborn feeling that if he warned her against Ted, then she would damn well go out with him because the last thing she needed was Nick Papaeliou's misguided good intentions.

She had been tormented by the thought that he and his leggy redhead had probably chuckled at the silly little woman in the short black dress who was clueless to the ways of the world. That, as much as anything else, had driven her to pick the phone up and dial one of the several numbers Ted had left with her.

She had said she would be going to Angelo's Pizza Emporium with Ted Splice and she would go to Angelo's Pizza Emporium with him if only to prove a point to herself. That she was a free woman, liberated from the chains of fear that had kept her anchored all her life. Nick, she had decided as she had got dressed earlier, making sure to wear clothes that wouldn't give Ted the wrong impression, might well turn out to be just the first in a long line of many.

She had been tempted to telephone Lily on the other side of the world and inform her of this new departure, a whole brand-new set of moral codes, but Lily had failed to show the appropriate disgust at Nick's high-handed behaviour at the party and had just laughed when accused of not coming to her rescue. She had departed for America still clinging to the belief that everything was going to be fine, just wait and see.

Now, sitting in the pizza emporium, which was truly an emporium and one that seemed unnaturally full of rowdy children, Rose was in danger, not of dodging Ted's wandering hands, but of nodding off through boredom.

Ted was not only very, very fond of the sound of his own voice and enchanted with all the funny stories he had up his sleeve, but he had also confided, on the way over in the taxi, lowering his voice, as if the cab driver could care less, that his inclinations were not entirely of the straight variety.

Of course, he adored women, but…

Rose had nodded and resigned herself to an evening of listening to Ted's anecdotes and looking at her watch.

At least the place was big so that they could manage to avoid a falsely intimate setting, and once or twice, as she nibbled at her pizza and salad, she actually found herself laughing at some of the wild things he had to say.

Apparently he found her *cool* and refreshing because she was such a good listener.

'If you were a guy,' he paid the highest compliment, 'then I'd be wining and dining you and inviting you back to my place to…'

'Look at your etchings?'

Which brought them right back to square one, the main subject for the evening, Ted himself, and his trials and tribulations as an artist before he had discovered his true calling behind the lens of a camera.

It was a little after ten by the time Ted asked for the bill.

'Been a bit of a waste for you, hasn't it?' he said sheepishly. 'I should have let you know…told you where my preferences lay…'

Rose laughed and impulsively reached across the table and held both his hands in hers. 'I just don't understand why you don't come out of the closet. It's the twenty-first century, after all, and you work in a world where it's pretty much the norm, anyway.'

'Oh, it's my mum, babe. Don't think she'd be too hip to the idea and, well…she's getting on a bit… Gotta play the respect card, man, gotta play the respect card.'

'Well, if this helps at all, I was playing a part that night as well.'

'You mean…'

'Oh, no! Not that.' Rose threw back her head and laughed, then she leaned forward and whispered confidentially, 'I'm actually a closet introvert. But last Saturday, I dressed to impress and played the part.'

'Well, now we know each other's wicked secrets, I think we're going to be friends for life.'

It was turning out to be an okay evening after all, Rose considered as they stood up, and when he slipped his arm around her waist she was quite happy to nestle against him and not at all offended when they parted company on the pavement outside, after promising that they would meet up again, maybe in a couple of months time, because Ted's schedule was 'like hectic, man'.

She washed her face, kicked off the high shoes and changed into her very un-wild gear of grey track-suit jogging bottoms and a sloppy tee shirt with a faded picture of Minnie Mouse on the front.

Heartbreak had, at least, had one good side effect. Her eating habits had changed. She had lost her appetite and it had conveniently failed to return so as she sat down to finish what remained of the evening in front of a bowl of carrot sticks and some low-fat dip she rested safe in the knowledge that the pizza was not going to be accompanied by a great slab of comfort-eating chocolate.

It took her fifteen minutes of surfing the channels before she landed on one that was watchable.

It would pass the rest of the evening, she supposed. No point heading up to bed because she knew that she would be unable to sleep. It had been the same for ages. She would close her eyes, will herself to think of something mundane, like what Annie at work had done with the reports she had laboriously redone three days ago, or what would be the next stage in her programming to update the Accounts Receivables department, and then she would think of him.

He sprang into her head like sweet temptation and forbidden fruit wrapped up in one agonisingly dangerous package. And he would always be laughing at her. Mostly, he would be laughing at her while rolling around in the bed with the redhead.

She was sipping some of the green tea with lemon that she had made to drink with her carrots and dip when the doorbell rang. She consulted her watch and frowned—nearly eleven-thirty on a Saturday evening.

Much as she had ended up enjoying her evening out with Ted, she hoped it wasn't him. She was certain that she would see him again because, as she wryly acknowledged, he enjoyed talking and in the field in which he worked so did nearly everyone else, she suspected, so a good listener was a valuable find. He had also shared a major confidence with her and that, in itself, would be a strong bond between them. All very nice, but she was looking forward to an hour or so of mindless television, drifting in and out of thoughts of Nick.

She tried to wipe the disgruntled expression from her face as she went to open the front door. She was pretty much prepared to give Ted one cup of coffee, but really nothing else. His urge to confide would have to wait for a more convenient hour.

But when she pulled open the door, it wasn't Ted hovering on her doorstep. It was Nick. Rose was so startled that she remained speechless for a few heart-stopping seconds. It seemed that he made a habit of appearing on her doorstep and sending her into a state of paralysing confusion.

'What are you doing here?' she demanded coldly. 'You can't keep just turning up on my doorstep, Nick.'

'Are you going to invite me in?'

'No.'

'Why not?'

'Because I have better things to do than talk to you.'

'Aren't you dressed in the wrong clothes for the better things you have in mind?' Wrong approach. This wasn't how things were meant to develop, not that he knew quite how things were meant to develop. He had just known, when he had seen them walking out of the restaurant, wrapped around each other like a couple on the way to the altar, that he had to do something. He couldn't just turn his back and walk away because he would be haunted by her for the rest of his life and that was a consequence he had no intention of accepting. He needed to get her out of his system and he wasn't going to achieve that by antagonising her.

'I have no idea what you're talking about,' Rose informed him, her voice cooling by several degrees. 'And I don't like your attitude.'

'I apologise.'

'What?'

'I apologise. I can see your point of view. I show up here, uninvited and unannounced, without so much as a bunch of flowers or a box of chocolates…'

Rose felt the colour crawl into her skin. She didn't know what was going on but there was a lazy warmth in his eyes that made her shiver with a horrible excitement, which she tried valiantly to slap down.

'What's going on, Nick? Why would you bring me flowers or chocolate?'

'Let me in, Rose. Give me a chance to explain.' It was an effort keeping his voice smooth and even and controlled because his only thought was that Ted the reformed producer was lurking somewhere inside her house, probably in her bedroom. True, women on the threshold of a rampant affair didn't usually deck themselves out in track suit bottoms and what looked like an ancient tee shirt from when she was a kid, but who was he to tell? The woman was a law unto herself.

Poor, hapless Ted wouldn't have known what he was letting himself in for when he decided to make a play for her. He would have been expecting a sexy version of the bimbos who littered the movie world. Rose must have come as a nasty surprise. Nick was tempted to smirk at the thought, but he contained himself and did his utmost to look penitent.

Rose, conversely, was looking back at him with deep, unhidden suspicion.

'It's late.'

'I know and I'm sorry about that.'

'Stop apologising, Nick. It doesn't suit you.'

Nick shot her a winning smile. 'You're right. It doesn't. Let me come in?'

'Oh, for goodness' sake.' She swung open the door and he walked past her into the hallway and then turned around so that he could subject her to another of those sexy smiles that made her head spin.

'Go and sit in the lounge and I'll bring you some coffee,' she said, just to get rid of him while she gathered her composure in privacy somewhere.

Flowers? Chocolate? She had no idea what he was playing at, but it had sent her into a tailspin. Even as she bustled around in the small kitchen, making him his mug of coffee, she was acutely aware of him sitting in her lounge, just a matter of a few metres away. Whatever he was up to, she thought firmly, she was having none of it. She reminded herself that he had a girlfriend. A bright, sparkling, picture-perfect model with limited vocabulary. Just the kind of woman he was inevitably drawn to, never mind his brief diversion with her. And anyway, she was a free and liberated young woman now, no longer hiding behind routine and safety to protect her from the big, bad world.

She found him obediently sitting where she had told him to sit, doing nothing more offensive than flicking through one of the computer magazines she liked to read occasionally, just to make sure that she was keeping in touch with the latest technology. He closed it as soon as she entered the room and handed him the coffee.

'Interesting reading material,' he commented. Well, at least the rehabilitated producer was not on the premises. Either that or he didn't mind going into hiding for an indefinite period of time.

'Why have you come?'

'How did your date go?'

'As you can see, I'm sitting here in one piece so your fears about Ted were misplaced.' And little do you know by how much, Rose thought wryly. 'Is that why you came? Your over-developed sense of duty kicking in again? Compelled to make sure that I wasn't cruelly taken advantage of and left sobbing somewhere on my own?'

'No.'

Rose felt confused once again. 'Then why?'

'I…I'm not very good at admitting things like this, but I didn't like seeing you with other men last week at that party.'

She held onto her common sense as tightly as she could and remembered the vital truth, which was that this man was not interested in a proper relationship with her or anyone else for that matter. Which brought her neatly to the redhead.

'I'm surprised you even noticed me, Nick. Wasn't your attention on your date?'

'You know it wasn't,' Nick said huskily.

'You mean you brought a woman to Lily's party when you weren't even interested in her?'

'So it would appear.'

'Why?'

'Because I thought she might be able to make me forget that I'm still attracted to you. It didn't work.' Nick rested his mug on the table in front of him and strolled over to the sofa where Rose was curled at one end with her feet tucked under her. 'Because I am—still attracted to you. Believe me, I don't want to be, but I can't help myself.' He decided he would keep the little mortifying fact that he had spent the evening spying on her to himself. Confession might be good for the soul but total cleansing was downright stupidity.

'Have you missed me?' he asked roughly.

'I… This is mad…'

'Have you? I've been going crazy thinking about you, Rose. Ever since last weekend, I've been going even crazier thinking about you and another man.' He took her hand in his, stroked her palm with his finger and then, devastatingly, kissed the soft, tender flesh.

It was like being burnt and Rose gasped and half closed her eyes.

This was all wrong. Playing the field was one thing when it was a journey of discovery. Playing the field with this man was no journey of discovery. She had discovered way too much on this particular journey.

But when he was leaning over her like this…telling her all this stuff…opening up and whispering how much he had missed her…

She let him scoop her legs onto his lap, knowing that she should be pulling away. The redhead, he was telling her now, had barely impacted on him. In fact he hadn't contacted her since the party and hadn't slept with her. She didn't turn him on. Not as *she*, *Rose*, *did*. Music to her ears.

'I've dreamt about your body, Rose…your ripe, sexy body. I've dreamt about your breasts…'

In response to that, Rose felt her breasts harden, disobeying all the strict rules she was laying down in her head about sticking to her guns.

'Will you let me touch them?'

'No,' she said weakly.

'Things didn't end between us, Rose, and you know it as well as I do.'

'It wouldn't work, Nick.'

'Sex between us can't fail to work.'

'That's not what I'm talking about.'

She tried to wriggle her legs into a more dignified position, a position more in keeping with a woman in control of her own mind and body. However, her legs had turned to jelly. Worse, they were obeying someone else's commands, and when he ran his hand lightly along her inner thigh they fell apart, willing slaves to whatever he wanted to do.

'You tell me that you're breaking away from the shackles that kept you locked up…' His voice was low and seductive and his hands were now doing even more inappropriate things, slipping under the elasticated waistband of her jogging bottoms, easing them lower so that he could caress her stomach. 'Break away with me, Rose.'

'You should go.'

'If you said it like you meant it, then I would.' His hand left her stomach to explore upwards now, until he was cupping her breast. No bra. This was his very own wet dream. 'But you don't want me to…' He touched the tip of her nipple, which was hard, and felt her sharp release of breath. 'You want me to do this… Do you want me to do more? Do you want me to suck those big, rosy nipples?' He flicked up the baggy tee shirt and this time it was his turn to inhale as he saw the vision that had been playing in his head ever since they had last made love.

'No…yes…no…I don't know…'

He did know. He recalled how much she loved him playing with her breasts and he began to suckle one of the rosy circles, loving the taste of her and hungry for more, like a starving man suddenly sitting at a banquet. As he sucked and pulled her nipple into his mouth his tongue flicked and darted over the sensitised tip, sending her into wild throes of abandon.

Somehow their bodies moved in harmony with one another, until she was sitting up, with her head flung back and Nick positioned kneeling between her legs so that he could lavish all his attention on her breasts.

He licked his way down and pulled down the jogging bottoms along with her underwear in one smooth, swift movement.

With his fingers, he parted the delicate folds of her and inserted his tongue, wriggling it towards the honeyed sweetness of the little bud that throbbed and begged for satisfaction.

And Rose accordingly groaned and lifted her hips off the sofa, tensing every muscle in her body as his questing tongue flicked and teased and his mouth tasted every inch of her most private parts.

She reached down to try and push him away and reclaim some of her will-power, and felt her fingers curl in his dark hair, urging him to bring her to completion right here, right now.

But Nick needed more than that and he couldn't wait. He was barely aware of taking off his clothes until he was standing in front of her, big and proud. Rose opened her eyes drowsily and smiled before reaching out and taking his throbbing member in her hand, where she proceeded to give it the same attention that he had given her.

Yes, she had missed this too. Missed him and missed touching him, missed the way her hands and mouth could turn this impressive, powerful man to putty.

By the time he drove into her, they were both so close to coming that it just took a few deep, urgent thrusts to send them tipping over the edge.

Rose recovered to the dull, depressing knowledge that she had made the same mistake. She had allowed her body to do what it wanted to while her brain trailed along somewhere far behind, raising its weedy objections.

The sofa felt cramped and uncomfortable. 'I need to go and get cleaned up,' she said, and Nick, catching onto the tone of her voice and hearing the shutters begin to slide into place, turned to her and frowned.

'You're not regretting what we just did, are you?'

'We're back to square one, Nick.'

'We need one another.' She was making to stand up and he yanked her back down so that she fell onto his lap where he could easily keep her prisoner. 'You didn't hear what I said, Rose. I missed you. I missed you from the minute we parted company at the airport and I haven't stopped.'

'Which is why you felt the need to replace me.'

'I told you, I thought I needed distraction. I was wrong. I need you. I need this. And so do you. You can say whatever you want, Rose, but your sweet, sexy body tells another story.'

'It tells a different story. I want you, and, yes, I was weak, but I want more than just sex.'

'Then come live with me.' Nick uttered the words, but they failed to evoke the horror he might have expected. He had never lived with a woman in his life before, but right now it didn't seem such an outlandish proposition.

To Rose, his proposal, noble though it was, especially for a man like him, was a halfway measure driven by lust. Love would have demanded a proposal of quite a different nature. Nick wanted her, but he also wanted to keep his options open. Boredom, for him, was lurking just around the corner and he was canny enough to realise that dumping a wife was completely different from dumping a live-in lover.

And, Lord, it was tempting. Tempting to think of having this bliss, but the inevitable rider of 'for however long it lasted' was too much of a threat to her peace of mind.

'No.'

'What do you mean *no*?' Nick looked at her in stunned surprise. He wasn't even aware of her standing up and sticking on her clothes. 'What do you mean *no*? Have you any idea what sort of a leap a commitment like that takes for a man like me? To have a woman share my space?'

'And I appreciate it…'

'But you really want marriage.' He was incredulous. He had just offered her something beyond the reach of every other woman he had ever known and she wanted more.

'I really do.' Rose took a deep breath and decided that there was no point playing any more games. She sat on the side of the sofa and looked at him carefully. 'You told me that you never wanted to carry on *wanting* me. Well, Nick…' she shot him a rueful smile '…I never wanted to fall in love with you, but I did. That's why I want to marry you. You tell me that we're sexually compatible. I tell you that we're compatible in far more ways than that. I tell you that we have what it takes. So…*will you marry me*?' Rose could actually feel the hammering of her heart. If someone had asked her to do a bungee jump off the Clifton Suspension Bridge, she couldn't have felt more terrified than she did at this very moment, but what was the use trying to keep the truth to herself any longer? Pride and dignity was all well and good, but if she walked away without telling him how she really felt it would haunt her for the rest of her life. She would always wonder what if, and 'what if's were too closely related to 'if only's for her liking.

Nick looked at her, aghast.

Love? Marriage? He couldn't contemplate it. Freedom of movement was so deeply ingrained in him that the thought of relinquishing it was unthinkable.

And, anyway, since when did women do the proposing?

He felt a surge of anger that she just hadn't been able to accept his already extreme sacrifice of moving in with him.

'Don't worry answering,' Rose said neutrally. She stood up and walked towards the door. 'Your answer's written on your face.' Now, she couldn't look at him, so instead she stared out into the hallway, hearing him get dressed and then feeling him move towards her.

'I'm not the marrying type of man. You always knew that, Rose. Why couldn't you have just accepted the parameters and appreciated the fact that I asked you to live with me? It's as good as…'

Rose took a deep breath and looked at him. She had her arms folded and she could feel her fingernails pressing painfully into her forearms. If they weren't she was sure that she would be shaking like a leaf. 'Because,' she said calmly, and where that dreadful calm came from she had no idea, 'marriage is all about commitment. Real commitment. Not just the "yes, let's stay together while the going's good" variety.'

'My commitment's always been to my work,' Nick told her

baldly. 'You're the closest I have ever come to sharing myself with another human being, but marriage…'

'Just one step too far?' Rose laughed mirthlessly and walked towards the front door.

There was a flat, cold feeling inside her, but, strangely, she was still glad that she had said what she had said, given it her best shot, so to speak. She didn't think he would be back now. In his mind, he would have opened a Pandora's box and, having slammed the lid back shut, he would never make the mistake of reopening it.

'We could have had fun.' His voice was cold and accusatory.

Rose shrugged and opened the door. 'Have a good life, Nick.'

She didn't watch him leave. Instead she closed the door quietly and leaned against it. She could hear the deep revving of his car as he pulled away from the kerb and then the sound of the engine was replaced by silence and she made her way up the stairs, into the bathroom, so that she could have a shower.

When she lay in bed, she replayed in her head this last night spent together. Before, even in the aftermath of Borneo and thinking that things were finally over for good, there had been, she realised now, an element of hope and a certain restless dissatisfaction. Now, there was closure. It made her neither happy nor unhappy. She just felt dead inside.

Life would carry on and it did. On the surface, Rose functioned as she always had. Competent and reliable at work, sociable enough with her circle of friends.

Breaking out of the mould was well and truly abandoned. The only surprise was her sister's reaction. Lily was disproportionately upset at the turn of events and that touched Rose.

'You'll get over it, Lily,' she laughed wryly down the phone. 'And so will I. In a year's time, we'll both see this as just another experience in the great adventure that is life.' She couldn't stand the thought that the damage done was irreparable. Surely not. Broken hearts mended, didn't they? Every magazine assured her of that.

But six weeks down the road, and Rose still found it hard to find a way through the dense fog of misery. She felt like a robot, going through the motions while underneath everything wilted and shrivelled away and died.

She had no idea what Nick was doing and she avoided buying any tabloids just in case she was tempted to open up those scurrilous gossip pages where she might see a picture of him cavorting with another redhead, mark two. Mark one might have been a distraction, but mark two would certainly have been the truly-narrow-escape replacement.

In the midst of this never-ending battle with her torn emotions and the sheer effort needed to carry on going to work, socialising with friends and pretending that all was well in the world of Rose Taylor, the dawning realisation that something else was very wrong took a little while to filter through.

When it did, the fragile glue that was binding her daily life together dissolved like wax in a flame and the truly sickening question reared its ugly head.

What on earth was she to do now?

CHAPTER TEN

Rose was on her way up to see him. Right now. At three in the afternoon. Right here. In his office.

Nick had no idea what she wanted. It had been nearly two months since he had set eyes on her and he had daily told himself that her disappearance from his life was the best thing that could have happened. He told himself that he had offered her the unthinkable and she had turned him down, proving his theory that women, each and every one of them, were out to change the men they purported to care about.

He had replayed countless times in his head that moment when she had told him that she was in love with him. If she were in love with him, he thought, why couldn't she have accepted what he had offered?

Because her aim had been to turn him into the domesticated animal that he was not and never would be.

It was a source of constant and relentless frustration that he still couldn't dismiss her from his head, where she had taken up residence and refused to budge.

He knew that his work was being affected. Not his ability to work, which was part and parcel of the essence of him, but his demeanour at work.

More than once he had been tempted to call her, but he

hadn't and he never would. Pride would never allow him to pick up that phone and dial her number.

But, and this was the thought that haunted him late at night when there was nothing to distract him, he longed for her. He wanted her loving him. He missed her. And he didn't know why.

Now his secretary had buzzed up that there was a certain Rose Taylor in reception, asking if she could come up and see him, and for the first time in weeks Nick felt a curious sense of peace. He immediately told his secretary that he was busy, that she might have to wait for half an hour while he wrapped up his conference call, but that he could squeeze her in after that.

Okay, it was childish of him, but she had always managed to turn him into a kid.

Then he sat back in his massive black leather chair, swivelled it to face the floor-to-ceiling plates of glass that overlooked the city of London, and turned his mind to what she wanted.

It could only be one thing. She had had ample time to think about his proposal and she had come to her senses. Nick contemplated the idea with intense satisfaction. He would even be tempted to say that he felt elated. He would have her back in his life, would have her sharp wit and clever mind and sexy body, and there would be no more talk about trying to infiltrate his life by putting a ring on his finger.

She loved him. Of course she would return. It was to be expected and Nick felt warm with the anticipation of having her back. Course, he would have to make it clear that his views hadn't changed. That a mistress was a far cry from a wife and matrimony was not on the agenda, but he didn't anticipate a problem.

After forty minutes, he buzzed through to his secretary to tell her that she could send Rose up now, and then he relaxed back, facing the heavy door to his office, and waited for her to enter.

'You've lost weight,' were his opening words as Rose cautiously entered his office and shut the door behind her.

She had prepared herself for this, but all her hours of preparation now flew out the window as she looked at him, despairingly aware that he still had as much of an effect on her now as he had the last time she had seen him. So much for time and its great healing properties.

Not wanting to leave the door because it represented her fastest route out, Rose remained hovering where she was, not quite sure how to answer his frowning observation, until he told her to have a seat. He actually stood up, pointed to the chair facing his and then proceeded to perch on the side of the desk so that she was forced to sidle forwards and sit at an awkward angle to avoid contact with his thigh.

'Well?' he demanded. 'Haven't you been eating?'

'I haven't come here to talk about my diet, Nick,' Rose answered irritably. She was aware that she was fiddling with the hem of her skirt and made herself stop. Nervous gesture. But she had a lot to be nervous about. In fact, she had spent the past two weeks in a state of near panic. Ever since she had clocked that she had missed a period. Ever since she had gone to the chemist's and bought one of those home pregnancy kits that were virtually one-hundred-per-cent accurate, leaving no doubt that she was well and truly pregnant with Nick's baby. That last time—no contraception. It had been wild and spontaneous and, unlike the very first time they had made love when they had omitted to use contraception, she hadn't been in her safe period.

And, yes, she had lost weight. She hadn't been eating properly and although, standing naked in front of the mirror, she could see that her stomach was more rounded, everywhere else was skinny in comparison to the curvy woman she had been. Who needed diets to lose weight? A healthy dose of misery worked a treat.

Not that she would look thinner for much longer.

She closed her eyes and felt suddenly dizzy. It was a good thing that she was sitting down. Collapsing on his office floor would have been a very disadvantageous way to begin proceedings.

'What's the matter?' Nick frowned because for a minute there he had actually thought that she was going to faint. Something kicked hard inside him, some inarticulate fear that she was ill. He removed himself back to his chair and tried to get himself together, because once that thought had inserted itself in his head it began to eat away at his logic, burrowing away until he was consumed with the conviction that there was something ominous that she was keeping from him.

For the first time since she had been announced, Nick entertained the possibility that she might not have come to his office because she wanted to engineer a reconciliation.

He had been on a high, anticipating her stammering admission that she couldn't keep away from him. He had even begun playing with thoughts of how the rest of his day would pan out. At his place. Uninterrupted sex. Touching her, feeling her, enjoying the things she could do to his body and all the myriad things he could do to hers.

But, now she was sitting in front of him, he could see that she was pale. This was not the demeanour of a woman looking forward to embarking on a heady and fulfilling sexual relationship with a man.

In fact, this was the demeanour of a woman who was nervous about blurting out an uncomfortable truth. Nick, astute when it came to reading other people, felt something shift inside him. He was scared, terrified in fact.

Everything seemed to slow down and he became uncomfortably aware that he had broken out in nervous perspiration. He could barely ask the question he knew he had to.

'Would you like something to drink? Tea? Coffee? I could ask my secretary to bring you some…'

Just the thought of tea or coffee made Rose feel nauseous. She went a couple of shades paler and shook her head.

'I won't be long, Nick,' she said, clearing her throat and making an effort not to be pathetic.

'No rush. Mind if I have a cup of coffee?' He buzzed through to his secretary to bring him in a cappuccino and Rose smiled wanly at him.

'Since when do you ask permission for anything, Nick?'

Since he wanted to buy some time before he heard what she had to say?

He was increasingly convinced that there was something seriously wrong with her. She looked terrible. As white as a sheet. And not because she was nervous, even though she clearly was. No, there was something underlyingly wrong, and as something close to terror continued to eat away at him Nick realised, in a moment of truth, what he had been missing all along.

He had let his own stubborn pride dictate his life. Nick Papaeliou, the man who could have any woman he desired, who had lived his life taking his pick and telling himself that his freedom was the most important thing he possessed, had clung to his vow never to commit like an idiot clinging to a lifebelt in a bath. No woman had ever been able to tempt him out of his conviction that bachelordom was the only way to go and so, when Rose had come along, he had steadfastly ignored all the glaring signs that had gradually begun to clutter his life.

He had mistaken his missing her when she wasn't around as missing her body. He had longed for her and explained it away as just a normal red-blooded-male reaction to craving a woman who turned him on. And when he had offered her the epitome of commitment as far as he was concerned, the chance to share his house with him, he had blithely assumed that the gesture signified no more than a desire to have what he wanted on tap until he became bored, until they both became bored.

Women had always eventually bored him and the fact that Rose was not included in that category had been so obvious from the start and yet so easy to ignore.

He could have kicked himself.

She had told him that she loved him and what had he done? Asked her to prove it by doing the one thing she didn't want to do: move in with him.

And now here she was and it sure as hell wasn't to set that particular little situation right.

She was here to tell him…what?

That she was ill. Thinking about that possibility made him feel instantly sick when his cappuccino was brought in and placed on the desk in front of him.

She was trying hard to be brave and meet his eyes, but she physically couldn't. He could see that and it terrified him.

'I can't have this conversation with you in my office,' he told her abruptly, and that, at least, made her raise her eyes and look at him.

'But you don't know what I'm going to say.'

'I know it's serious, whatever it is.' He pushed the coffee away from him and stood up.

Rose failed to follow suit. Instead she watched as he slung on his jacket, her fists pressed into her lap.

'I don't want to go anywhere, Nick. I want to say what I have to say here. Where it's impersonal…'

Nick shot her a brooding, sideways glance and hesitated before removing his jacket and carefully replacing it on its hanger. Then he walked towards the window and stared down at the city streets below, trying to get his thoughts in order, filled with a cold, clawing panic and the painful knowledge that he had to say what he had to say before she unleashed whatever truth it was she had come to impart to him.

He could feel her eyes on him and, sure enough, he turned around to find her watching him.

'Look,' he began, 'I'm…I don't know how to say this…' He raked his fingers through his hair and shook his head, suddenly restless and uncomfortable. 'I've never said this to anyone before…'

Rose, having screwed up every ounce of courage she possessed to tell him what she had to and as quickly as possible, breathed a silent sigh of relief that he was doing the talking. Okay, it was just a case of putting off the inevitable and it was cowardly, but she relaxed just a tiny bit.

She was also curious, even though she didn't want to be. She hadn't come to his office expecting to have a conversation, or at least not until she had told him about the pregnancy and then conversation probably wouldn't quite describe what she imagined would follow. Recriminations, accusation, bitterness—nothing that she would classify as conversation.

'Said what?' she asked, bewildered.

Even more bewildering was the expression on his face. Gone was the easy self-assurance she associated with him. In its place was uncertainty and hesitation, which was as perplexing as the dark flush that stained his cheeks.

She almost forgot what she had come to say when he walked towards her and dragged his chair round so that he could position himself right next to her, on her level.

'I…' he began. 'I…I'm glad you're here…'

He didn't look glad. In fact, he didn't look anything, at least not anything she could identify. And if he really was glad, then she was pretty sure that it wasn't a sentiment he would be harbouring for very long.

'I…the past few weeks, Rose…' He once again ran his fingers through his hair and looked away from her. 'Not good.'

In a flash, she knew where he was going. He had probably assumed that she had come to his office with a view to taking him up on his offer for her to live with him and was now, against the dictates of his pride, going to repeat the offer because he still wanted her. Want, want, want! The most distasteful and egotistical word in the universe.

She closed her mind off to her memories of him. It gave her strength to think that this man, whatever he said, hadn't wanted her enough to take their relationship that one important step further. She had declared her love and that, psychologically, must have led him to assume that she would return, grateful for the crumbs he could throw her.

'I'm not here to talk about that,' she interjected quickly.

'You don't understand, Rose. I need to talk about it. I need to talk about what a fool I've been.' He reached out and took hold of her fingers, idly playing with them, obviously, she thought, unaware of what that simple, inoffensive gesture was doing to her insides. She stared, fascinated and dry-mouthed, at his long brown fingers as they fiddled with hers, and gulped.

It was amazing that he couldn't guess the reason for her visit. Astute as he was, his mind was obviously not programmed to think the unthinkable.

'I let you go,' he said quietly, looking directly at her. 'I let the woman who loved me go.'

Rose didn't want to be reminded of that. 'I'm not here to blame you, Nick. You did what you had to do and there are no hard feelings. I haven't come to discuss the past.' She made an effort to slide her hand out of his grasp but his fingers tightened on hers, clasping them into submission.

'I've always thought that love was a complication, something of which I had no need. I enjoyed women but I didn't want them clambering into my private life and interfering with it. My goals were set and there was no place for cosy nights in and joint holidays in Italy with the eventual two point two.'

Which snapped Rose back to the present like a bucket of cold water.

'No. I gathered,' she said coolly.

'I was…mistaken…'

It took a couple of seconds for his words to sink in, then her thoughts were adrift, bobbing about in confusion as she tried to assimilate that telling, wrenched remark.

'I…beg your pardon?'

'I was mistaken,' Nick said simply. He felt a weight lift off his chest. Whatever dire news she had come to break, then she would know how he felt and it was something he should have said a long time ago. Courage, he was discovering, was something he had measured using all the wrong tools. Courage was this. Telling the only woman he had ever loved that he loved her.

Rose wasn't sure what she was hearing. She knew what she wanted to hear.

'You're playing games,' she said uncertainly. 'Please.' This time she succeeded in withdrawing her hand, which she held up because, riveting though his disclosures were, she couldn't trust herself not to start believing them, and hadn't he already made it perfectly clear that he was not in the business of love? What would he do to get her back into his bed? she wondered. Seduce her with words he knew she wanted to hear?

No. She would say what she had come to say and watch him fall back in horror. Better that than to be lulled into a false sense of security that would be snatched away the minute she broke her news.

'Just listen to me and stop…confusing me.'

Nick had the cold feeling that he had left things too late. The horse had bolted and, not only had he failed to realise what a treasure he possessed, but he had closed the stable door and returned to the house whistling a merry tune. He deserved to have her walk out on him and never look back. His punishment would be to spend the rest of his life living with his mistake.

'I…' Now it was her turn to stammer. She took a deep breath and said in one quick rush, closing her eyes to block him out, 'I'm pregnant. I'm sorry. I didn't mean for it to happen, but it has. You don't have to feel responsible. You don't have to feel anything. I came here because I felt you ought to know, not because I wanted anything from you. You're telling me now about mistakes, but I know you for who you are. I don't want money from you; I don't want time from you. I just thought…you should know…'

In a minute she would do the brave thing and open her eyes. The silence lengthened around them and into it she read an assortment of reactions. Eventually, though, she peeped at him and then opened her eyes fully when she realised that he hadn't drawn back in horror.

'You're pregnant?'

'I'm sorry,' Rose whispered.

'You're pregnant.'

'I realise this is the last thing you want…'

'I don't believe it.' Nick shook his head in wonderment. It had never occurred to him. How naïve was he? He had lurched from thinking that she had returned because she wanted him, to imagining the worst, that she was ill, perhaps fatally so. But she was carrying his child and he was overwhelmed with a sudden feeling of elation.

He looked at her and grinned.

'You're…not upset?' she asked cautiously.

'You're having my baby…' He wanted to sweep her off her feet and swing her around. 'I love you, Rose. I love you, I can't live without you and now you've given me the best news I could ever have hoped for. Lord, when you walked through that door, with that serious expression, white like a ghost, I thought…I don't know what I thought…that you were going to tell me that you were ill…that I had lost my chance to show you how much you mean to me…'

Rose's brain had registered his declaration of love and had stuck there.

'If you loved me, why didn't you say something sooner?'

'Because I didn't understand myself.' Nick smiled wryly at her. 'You crept up on me and took over my soul and, like an idiot, I still thought that I was in control. When I heard that you had come here, my world fell into place again.'

'And what if I hadn't come here?' Rose was not going to allow hope to push her headlong over the precipice. 'Would you have let me disappear?'

'I could never have done that.' Nick thought about it, thought about his pride, realised that it would have lasted so long and then he would have woken up to the fact that he couldn't live without her. And he wasn't too proud, now, to tell her that and to delight in seeing her wariness finally melt away.

'And now I'm going to be a father…' God, he felt choked

up. 'Let's get out of here. I want to celebrate and then I want us to get married.'

'What, today?' Rose laughed.

'By the end of the week,' Nick growled. 'You need looking after and the sooner I get started, the better…'

HARLEQUIN *Presents*

He's successful, powerful—and extremely sexy....
He also happens to be her boss! Used to getting his
own way, he'll demand what he wants from her—
in the boardroom and the bedroom....

Watch the sparks fly as these couples
work together—and play together!

IN BED WITH
THE BOSS

REQUEST YOUR FREE BOOKS!

2 FREE NOVELS PLUS 2 FREE GIFTS!

YES! Please send me 2 FREE Harlequin Presents® novels and my 2 FREE gifts. After receiving them, if I don't wish to receive any more books, I can return the shipping statement marked "cancel." If I don't cancel, I will receive 6 brand-new novels every month and be billed just $3.80 per book in the U.S., or $4.47 per book in Canada, plus 25¢ shipping and handling per book and applicable taxes, if any*. That's a savings of close to 15% off the cover price! I understand that accepting the 2 free books and gifts places me under no obligation to buy anything. I can always return a shipment and cancel at any time. Even if I never buy another book from Harlequin, the two free books and gifts are mine to keep forever.

106 HDN EEXK   306 HDN EEXV

Name	(PLEASE PRINT)	
Address		Apt. #
City	State/Prov.	Zip/Postal Code

Signature (if under 18, a parent or guardian must sign)

Mail to the Harlequin Reader Service®:
IN U.S.A.: P.O. Box 1867, Buffalo, NY 14240-1867
IN CANADA: P.O. Box 609, Fort Erie, Ontario L2A 5X3

Not valid to current Harlequin Presents subscribers.

Want to try two free books from another line?
Call 1-800-873-8635 or visit www.morefreebooks.com.

* Terms and prices subject to change without notice. NY residents add applicable sales tax. Canadian residents will be charged applicable provincial taxes and GST. This offer is limited to one order per household. All orders subject to approval. Credit or debit balances in a customer's account(s) may be offset by any other outstanding balance owed by or to the customer. Please allow 4 to 6 weeks for delivery.

Your Privacy: Harlequin is committed to protecting your privacy. Our Privacy Policy is available online at www.eHarlequin.com or upon request from the Reader Service. From time to time we make our lists of customers available to reputable firms who may have a product or service of interest to you. If you would prefer we not share your name and address, please check here. ☐

HP07

I ♥ HARLEQUIN *Presents*

BROUGHT TO YOU BY FANS OF
HARLEQUIN PRESENTS.

We are its editors and authors
and biggest fans—and we'd
love to hear from YOU!

Subscribe today to our online blog at
www.iheartpresents.com

HARLEQUIN®

Mediterranean
NIGHTS™

This cruise is throwing her off balance...

Coming in April 2008...

STARSTRUCK

by
fan favorite
Michelle Celmer

When Claire Mackenzie is invited aboard
Alexandra's Dream by her grandfather—screen
legend Frederick Miles—she forgoes partying for
chaperoning his show rehearsals. She's convinced
that Liam Bates, the ship's charismatic assistant cruise
director, is trying to use her grandfather for his own
benefit. But as much as Claire thinks Liam's charms
are an act, she's having a tough time resisting them!

*Available wherever books are sold
starting the first week of April.*

Look for the exciting conclusion to
Mediterranean Nights, THE WAY HE MOVES by
Marcia King-Gamble, in May 2008.

HARLEQUIN *Presents*

THE *DESERT KINGS*

**Blood brothers, hot-blooded lovers—
who will they take as their queens?**

These sheikhs are blood brothers, rulers of
all they survey. But though used to impossible
wealth and luxury, they also thrive on the
barbaric beauty of their kingdom. Are there
women with spirit enough to tame these hard,
proud kings and become their lifelong queens?

THE SHEIKH'S
CHOSEN QUEEN
by *Jane Porter*

Jesslyn has been summoned to the desert land
Sheikh Sharif rules. Jesslyn refuses to take orders, but
Sharif is determined: she will obey his command and
submit—to becoming his wife and queen!

Available April 2008 wherever books are sold.

Look on Jane's Web site for more information
on this sizzling miniseries!

The big miniseries from

HARLEQUIN *Presents*

Dare you read it?

Bedded by *Blackmail*
Forced to bed...then to wed?

He's got her firmly in his sights and she's got
only one chance of survival—surrender to his
blackmail...and him...in his bed!

THE ITALIAN
RAGS-TO-RICHES WIFE
by Julia James
Book # 2716

Laura Stowe has something Allesandro di Vincenzo wants,
and he must grit his teeth and charm her into his bed, where
she will learn the meaning of desire....

Available April 2008 wherever books are sold.

Don't miss more titles in the
BEDDED BY BLACKMAIL series—coming soon!

www.eHarlequin.com

HPI2716